FOR-
Janet Fenton.
all good wishes
Billy Clark
2000

BY WAY OF THE

Forked Stick

Other Books by Billy C. Clark

A Heap of Hills

A Long Row to Hoe

Song of the River

Trail of the Hunter's Horn

Mooneyed Hound

Goodbye Kate

Useless Dog

The Champion of Sourwood Mountain

Riverboy

Sourwood Tales (short stories)

To Leave My Heart at Catlettsburg (poetry)

BY WAY OF THE

Forked Stick

Billy C. Clark

The University of Tennessee Press / Knoxville

First Edition.

The paper used in this book meets the minimum
requirements of ANSI/NISO Z39.48-1992 (R 1997)
(Permanence of Paper). The binding materials have
been chosen for strength and durability. Printed on
recycled paper.

Library of Congress Cataloging-in-Publication Data

Clark, Billy C. (Billy Curtis)
By way of the forked stick / Billy C. Clark.— 1st ed.
        p. cm.
ISBN 1-57233-094-5 (cl.: alk. paper)
1. Appalachian Region, Southern—Social life and
customs—Fiction. I. Title.
PS3505.L2425 B9 2000
813'.54—dc21   00-008431

To my wife, Ruth, who lived it with me

Contents

The Apache Pest Control

1

Most of what I knew about Apache, Weasel, and his woman, Lottie, was second-hand. It had come by way of my brother Caleb, Mom on occasion, the boys Caleb loafed-off with, and the old men who came to whittle on Saturdays at Kelsey May's general store in Sourwood. Most of what I heard was as mysterious and exciting as ghosts.

Apache owned and operated the APACHE PEST CONTROL in and about Sourwood. A time back, he had met, courted, and married Lottie Hager who was living at the time on Viney Branch. She had lived most of her life there taking care of her ailing mother and her shiftless brother, Weasel. Her mother had passed on a year before Apache met her; Weasel was there because of a death-promise Lottie had made to her mother to always see that Weasel had a good home. That Weasel went with the marriage hadn't bothered Apache at all, especially the way it turned out. Weasel was good to follow, mind, and do most of the work— doing most of the work being the way most everyone turned out if they fooled with Apache, and especially boys.

Mom said it was a pity Lottie got mixed up with him. Lottie was a good woman, a gospel woman. With Lottie spending most of her life waiting on an ailing mother and a shiftless brother, Apache had probably been the first man she had taken up with. Judging Apache a ne'er-do-well, Mom thought Lottie was more deserving, but the loneliness of the mountain brought about strange things. Apache and Weasel deserved one another; they were like two yolks inside the same egg.

Caleb said that Apache was like a spider: he'd coax you to his web and have you cocoon-tight before you knew it. Caleb didn't know the

1

name of a single boy Apache loafed with who hadn't worked for Apache at one time or the other. They had all ended up like Caleb: nothing to show for it. That Apache had magic attached to him.

Others said that the measurement for growing up on Sourwood Mountain did not begin until you had been lured, caught, and danced your time along the strands of the web as all older boys had done, and that caught and dancing was never a matter of "if" but "when." Apache was the high-water mark for swollen wants and the low-water mark for broken promises.

Even Mom said on more than one occasion practically the same thing whenever Apache's name was mentioned: there was a magic attached to him that drew boys off the mountain like a magnet. But as far as she knew, no harm had ever come to a boy because of it. In fact and unbeknownst to Apache she was sure, she had noticed some good coming from it: a growingupidish sort of good.

"He'll get you, too," Caleb warned, "especially with your head full of nothing but hound dogs. He can spot a boy's want a mile off. And with your want swollen enough to keep me awake nights talking about it, the time for web-casting has come."

Among the three of them only Lottie was called by her given name, although many people added on "the gospel woman." Apache had come by his nickname by claiming to be part Indian. And to be part Indian around Sourwood meant Apache; they were the only ones anyone had ever seen on the big screen at the picture show. A mean sort, always wanting to circle something and cause trouble. High-cheekboned and wind-tanned, he did look Indianish, especially if you wanted him to, which I did. The only thing that bothered me was his beard. Caleb said that Indians never grew beards and never had to bother about shaving like he did. Or had tried to once, I remembered, by stealing Dad's razor and almost ending up with a licking from Mom. She scolded and then grinned and told him that if he would put a little cream on his chin her cat would lick the fuzz off. I remembered that because Caleb told me later that if I let word out about what Mom had said that I could just mark off having a brother. But Sid Larkin told me that Apache having a beard didn't bother him at all; it probably came from the non-Indian side of his family. That made good sense. Sid wanted Apache to be part Indian, too.

Weasel's given name was Esau. Apache had pinned him with the nickname because he was wiggly, quick, and the best he had ever seen about getting in and out of tight places. Exactly what he needed for his termite business, but Mom said the name fit because Esau was as sneakin as a weasel.

Caleb could remember when Apache had started courting Lottie on Viney Branch. I had been there once with Caleb, and he had pointed out where Lottie had lived. The long wooden porch on the front of the house had fallen in and the little house, deserted now, had been taken over by varmints. We had gone of the winter to ice skate on the narrow branch that had gouged the hollow out of the mountain. The branch had enough slope to it so that you did not have to push yourself along the ice. The branch, frozen enough on top to hold our weight, was stretched out like a long, white ribbon. I could hear the current underneath slow-winding over rocks and threading the roots of sycamores stretched out like the legs of giant spiders. Willow limbs danced in the wind, and the naked tips of their limbs penciled strange designs on the lean tablets of snow along the edge of the ice. I watched as the cold wind snatched dry snow, whirled it into a cone, and sent it dancing ahead of us. I asked Caleb about coming back during the summer to turtle-noodle and seine for bait for our trotline. But he said the branch had too many copperheads for that. I never asked a second time.

Apache had gone up Viney Branch to drum for termite business, and he had met Lottie there. She had been standing on the long, wooden porch, cocooned inside a woolen coat that she forever wore and that was long enough to cover her ankles. She was catching what she could of a morning sun, sharing it with strings of threaded leatherbritches that she had hung to dry from the roof beams. A wind trembled the long strings of beans, and their shadows quivered on Lottie's lean body like dancing snakes. She was a tall, thin woman, Lottie was. Thin and forever cold. Pale as a wilted flower, she was not judged much to look at. But, later, after I had come to know her first-hand, she looked natural enough. And, like Mom had said, she was soft-hearted but always cold.

A gospel woman sure enough who spent most of her time reading scripture, searching for warmth, and set on seeing everyone on Sourwood Mountain "born again," especially boys.

Apache had offered Lottie a free termite job and took most of the summer doing it. He went there everyday, and of the evenings he sat with her on the long, wooden porch trying mostly to find a way to get shed of Weasel. But, Caleb said, if you had a weakness Apache would search it out. He found Weasel's. Weasel loved raw turnips, and Lottie had bushels stored in her root cellar. Pretending to love turnips too, Apache took to sending Weasel off to the root cellar. It had been Weasel's bragging about Apache courting Lottie down at Kelsey May's that had drawn Caleb and the boys he loafed with there, Caleb leading the pack. They hid off in the bushes hoping for a full moon to see and a windless night to hear. "It was during the time it took Weasel to get to the root cellar and back that was something," Caleb said, clicking his heels together. "Whoopee!"

Curious, I asked: "What do you mean, 'whoopee?'"

Caleb grinned.

"Just stay with trapping and hound dogs and leave the whoopee to me," he said. "I wouldn't go asking Mom about it either; it ain't apt to turn you a favor."

But I was too curious not to.

Mom grinned and then frowned.

"I guess he's growing faster than I wish he ought," she said. "But Caleb is right: best you stick with trapping but forget about a dog to feed. At least for now. Your time will come soon enough."

"But what did he mean by whoopee?" I asked.

When she spoke again it was as if she was not talking to me at all.

"Yes," she said, "there's hope for Caleb in your not knowing. He stopped far short of where I thought he would have on something like that."

I thought I heard her giggle as she walked off, leaving me more curious than ever.

I tried to smoke Caleb out.

"Did Weasel ever know?" I asked.

Caleb just acted like he never knew what I was talking about. "Know what?" he asked.

"What happened between Apache and Lottie while he was off to the root cellar," I said. "You know, whoopee."

"He wouldn't have known if Apache had spelled it out for him," Caleb laughed. "When it comes to women, he's as green as you. Never even knew that Apache never ate a turnip he brought back. Apache hates turnips. He just caught Weasel not looking and shucked them over the back of his chair where they gathered in a doodle."

"But didn't he know when morning came?" I asked.

"By the time Weasel was up, Lottie had already fed them to the hogs," Caleb said. "He didn't even know Apache and Lottie was married until it came time to move to Apache's place up Echo Hollow."

Poor Lottie! Moved to Echo Hollow, the longest, deepest, and darkest hollow gouged out of Sourwood Mountain. Squeezed by the mountain, the hollow was not much broader than a tramroad. On either side, the mountain was ridged as keen as a plow-point and looked high enough to furrow clouds. On either ridge, looking down, the hollow seemed no wider than a finger. So high up that it was scary to look down. But even more scary, I thought, to be in the hollow looking up. For each ridge seemed to bend inward, threatening to fold over you. And high up old cedars, twisted by wind and whitened by time, clung to the mountain with gnarled and feeble roots like bony fingers of old men. Crows cawed their lonesome song from ridge to ridge and turkey buzzards circled searching for something below. So scary that I had often sneaked off under the trees. There were too many scary tales about buzzards to suit me.

Early of the mornings a fog settled over and hung from the limbs of trees like a ghost-wash. When the morning grew old, and a meager sun came to wring the fog-wash like the hands of an old woman, drops of fog drip, dripped on the underbrush below like the tick of a clock. Moss quilted much of the low land, and over the mouth of deserted coal mines ice hung like white beards of old men, remaining long after spring had come to the rest of the mountain. What little sun came, worked its way slowly down the slopes and reached the low land as

5

feeble as a miner's lamp. Birds searched out the meager heat and sang feeble songs. Lottie gathered with them inside her long, woolen coat and gathered what heat she could. Cold and lonesome. Old-timers at Kelsey May's said that to come out of Echo Hollow was like going south. You could stand up the hollow and yell to the top of your voice, listen while your voice bounced off the slopes mournful and sad and then died. Old-timers said no voice ever made it out. A lonesome hollow with too many scary tales to count.

Old men whittling at Kelsey's said that Echo Hollow had at one time held the biggest and finest timber on Sourwood Mountain. Timber so tall that you couldn't shoot a squirrel from the top of it. Trees so large that a half-dozen men couldn't lock hands and reach around them. They told of how the men, snaking the huge logs out of the hollow, would stop at the mouth to cool their mules. And how they stood, caught in the coldest wind that ever came out of a hollow, their mouths frothing and quivering their hides to knock flies off that had been addled by the cold. It was a picture so real that sometimes when I stood in the mouth of the hollow, I could squint my eyes, and the brown stumps left from the giant trees became mules standing timeless, their heads hung, and their tails swishing, rocking their bodies back and forth as slow as the crawl of a turtle.

Lon Wills, an old-timer holding the record at Kelsey's for the longest shaving without breaking, told me once that Echo Hollow was bad for owls.

"How come?" I asked.

"Well," he said, shifting the cud of tobacco in his mouth, "it's the nature of owls to hoot at night and sleep during the day. But with daylight so slow coming to that hollow they just hoot until their voice becomes a whisper. Sad and funeral-like. It ain't all wind you hear in that hollow; it's the whisper of owls, mostly."

I asked Caleb once why anyone would want to live in the head of Echo—why Weasel and Lottie had agreed to go there, especially Lottie since she was cold all the time anyway.

"Simple," Caleb answered. "Lottie got herself man-crazy, which is the way all women get sooner or later. Weasel got three meals a day and a place to sleep, got his picture painted on the door of the big termite truck which made him important-like. With Apache it was termites and buying the hollow for little or nothing."

"Termites?" I asked. "How come?"

"They take to damp and dark places," Caleb said. "Plenty of both up Echo. And with so much old wood to eat they grow big and rowdy."

During the days that followed I found out that Caleb wasn't the only one who had picked up rumors about termites up there. Ren Dawkins, in the same grade as Caleb, said that Apache kept termites penned up in fruit jars up there, and that he fed them special things. That before long they grew so fast that he had to transfer them to pickling crocks. Said that he had seen a big one up there one day firsthand. He had been on the mountain hunting squirrels when Lottie had coaxed him down for tea. Not really wanting to go but afraid she might cast a spell on him if he didn't since he had heard she had powers, he joined her there in the yard. Before he had taken two swallows she was deep into the Book of Job. It had been somewhere during Job's troubles that he had heard the grinding noise. Squinting his eyes carefully so as to dodge Lottie's wrath and be forced to stay for Psalms, he watched the door to an outbuilding open slowly. With fire coming from Lottie's scripture and knowing of his short-comings, it could have been the devil but wasn't. Unable to move since to do so might heat Lottie more thinking that the Spirit was reaching him, he sat motionless and watched a huge termite, the size of a ground squirrel, lean against a doorjamb and chew on a singletree. Ren never figured to hunt that deep in Echo again.

The thing that added to the rumors on termites was the fact that Apache made no bones that he kept them up Echo. He kept them there to experiment on. Caged, he could watch their habits, feed them different woods, and douse them with several mixtures to see which worked best. He claimed that it was necessary to do that. For termites were as changeable as the weather; what snuffed one out today might drowsy or whet his appetite the next. Among other things, he had learned that a termite would play possum—act dead as a stump while you were there, but once you were gone, go back to eating twice as fast and twice as furious.

7

There were also rumors that followed Weasel. Lean and lizard-quick, he had taken to termites right off and, worse, they had taken to him, had a way of showing up wherever he had been. And you never knew when or where that might be. It could be at your house just at the break of day, casting around like he was spotting for termites. A shadow of a little man, tough as rawhide with beady eyes casting like a snake's tongue. His hands were always inside his pockets. If you were lucky, he was searching for a chew or a raw turnip—unlucky it might be a handful of termites. Ralph Jackson said that once Weasel was done, he could whistle them in like a pack of hounds and turn them loose somewhere else.

Caleb told me that if I ever caught Weasel casting about our house, to handle him as careful as a soft-craw. Doing so was no guarantee that he wouldn't drop termites off on you, but to be unneighborly was a sure bet. Weasel was quick to take offense and hold a grudge, especially since he had lost most of his power of smell and some of his sight on the side of Sourwood Mountain—a story that had two sides to it: the one I had heard from Caleb and the old-timers at Kelsey's and the one I heard from Mom. I liked the one from Caleb and the old-timers best; Mom's probably held more truth to it.

According to Caleb and the old-timers, Apache, Weasel, and a big hound that Apache had traded for called Geronimo had gone off on the mountain one night to see if they could catch Lottie a possum. Nothing pleased Lottie more than a possum fattened on persimmons and paw paws. Somewhere along the mountain, old Geronimo hit a track, trailed it only a short distance before barking holed. That the trail had been short was a good sign of possum. That the possum had taken to a hole instead of a tree was a sign that Geronimo had caught it out and had crowded it.

When they reached the hound, they saw that he had holed under a big sandstone rock, tall as a doodle of winter hay. The hole was large which meant that varmints had been using it for years. Weasel, knowing that varmints were smart and always made them a second hole for escape, worked his way around the rock to find it. He did—a hole larger than the one where Apache and Geronimo waited, so large that he thought he could work his shoulders inside it. He tried and did. With his shoulders through, he slid the rest of his body inside the hole like a snake—which now meant either one of two things: if he could reach the possum, it would more than likely sull, and he could grab it by its tail and pull it out, or if it tried to make a run for it, the possum would have to take the hole where Apache waited. Apache could simply hold the grass sack they had brought over the hole and scoop it up ahead of Geronimo. For to catch game was the hound's biggest flaw; he would run off down the mountain with it. He never wanted to give game up. And as bad to eat possum as Lottie. Weasel stretched out some and whispered toward Apache: "Hear me over there, Apache?"

Apache answered, "Loud and clear. Having a hard time holding this hound!"

"Then better get the sack over the hole and watch out!" Weasel whispered. "If he don't sull, he'll come your way."

"Fool if he does," Apache cackled.

While Weasel worked his way slowly deeper into the hole, Apache hunkered and scooped dirt from just inside the hole. He let the dust-dirt sift slowly through his fingers screening it with his carbide light. He watched closely for varmint hairs, hairs that would tell him what sort of varmints were using the hole now. It took only one handful: the hairs were as black as midnight. Apache backed off some and whispered: "Back off, Weasel! It's a polecat!"

Maybe Apache was too far from the hole now for Weasel to hear him; maybe he was too excited and caught up with the catch. Whichever, he whispered: "There he sits! It's black as midnight in here. Easy now. . . ."

Apache rolled up the sack to make sure nothing could get in it. The big hound had slipped off down the mountain at the first word of polecat.

"Back off I tell you," Apache whispered from still farther back. "It's a polecat!"

But all he heard was Weasel, coaxing.

"Easy now! Old Weasel ain't gonna hurt you."

Next, Apache heard Weasel's mournful yell. Maybe figuring that

9

the skunk might come out his side, and knowing that Weasel had the hole on that side blocked off, Apache made his way around the rock. When he reached there, all he could see were Weasel's brogans sticking out from under the rock. The smell of polecat lay on the land like a fog. Holding his breath, Apache grabbed Weasel's brogans, stretched Weasel's legs like rubber bands and popped him out of the hole. Leaving poor Weasel writhing on the ground, Apache cut a long sapling and shoved one end of it under Weasel's arms.

"I can't see!" Weasel wailed.

"Just feel." Apache answered. "Grab the end of the pole, and I'll lead you off the mountain."

"Send in the hound just in case the polecat comes after me!" Weasel said.

"Send the hound in, Hell!" Apache answered. "The sonofabitch is probably home by now which means that Lottie will know something is wrong and be watching. If we make it by Lottie this time, I'll trade that sonofabitch off after daylight!"

Down the mountain they went, Weasel on one end of the pole and Apache on the other. Snaked poor Weasel off the mountain as blind as Samson.

Apache was right. Geronimo stood beside Lottie wagging his tail.

"It's poor Weasel!" Apache yelled ahead. "I brung him home on the end of a pole!"

"Then you oughten to have any trouble polling him to the rain barrel while I fetch a bar of lye soap," she yelled back.

And while Weasel shivered and scrubbed in the cold water, Lottie lathered him down with scripture stronger than lye, from a distance.

By daylight, Weasel had lost his power of smell and, he claimed, some of his sight. Which made some sense, I thought; I had heard about more than one dog losing some or both after a direct hit from a polecat. Probably the same on people.

Mom's story was short and simple. She said that Apache and Weasel, unbeknownst to Lottie, had been off on the mountain again making moonshine that everyone knew they made and that their still had blown up.

"Do the devil's work," she said, "and draw the devil's pay."

Mom's story was no stranger around Kelsey's. A mention of it would bring smiles to the faces of the old-timers but no talk. But I had learned that their smiles often verified the truth of something.

2

Someone around Sourwood had named the big truck Apache drove "Thusla" because of its age. Behind the cab of the truck he had built a long, wooden bed and mounted two round metal tanks on it. A rubber hose was attached to each tank, and when not in use, they were coiled up like black snakes. On the right door Apache had had painted the picture of a giant termite stretched out on its back and about to be tomahawked by a giant of a man that everyone knew was Apache. Dribbled across the seam of the door was a smaller man pinning the termite with his knee, and everyone knew that was Weasel. One of the tanks was said to hold the exterminator for termites and the other the mixings from septic tanks that Apache pumped off for the uppities around Sourwood who had inside privies. The thing was, no one knew which tank held what; flies swarmed them both.

The truck had solid rubber tires and was as cantankerous about getting started as a mule. Up Echo, he always parked it on a rise and had Weasel shove it off each morning. And when Weasel got to complaining about his back, he traded for an old mare mule to help get it rolling. But Lottie had soon put a stop to that. Lottie claimed that the mule was so old that she had to soak corn for her before she could eat it, and besides the mule was the only company Lottie had most times close-up. The old mule stood mostly in the yard with her head hung repenting-like while Lottie rubbed her down with scripture.

On a job, Apache always tried to park on a grade. When he couldn't, he'd send Weasel off to find help to push. And everyone in Sourwood soon learned that if they saw Weasel waving his arms, it was time to hide-out. Almost everyone had pushed the big truck at least once, from old men to boys of all sizes. And the thing was, you might push for a mile, only to find out that Apache had forgotten to turn the key on! No matter, he sat on the inside comfortable-like, spurting encouragement and ambeer out the window.

3

The first time I really met Apache close-up, Caleb and I were in the yard splitting wood when we heard the big truck churning up the road. This side of the house, Apache parked the truck on a rise and killed the motor. I watched Apache and Weasel get out of the cab. Apache was grinning and looking straight at me; Weasel casted about with eyes quick as a lizard's tongue. Remembering what Caleb said about being neighborly, I tried to smile at him, but he never smiled back.

Caught between a mixture of sun and shadows, I thought Apache looked Indianish enough. He was a big man, rawboned and broad across the shoulders. His hair was long, straight, and black as midnight except for streaks of salt-white. I watched the wind play with his beard, and it moved back and forth like it had a life of its own. The beard still bothered me some, but his skin was reddish which I took to be natural instead of wind-made.

He walked toward us with Weasel behind carrying a poke. When Apache was close enough, he reached out his long arm and placed a hand on top of my head. I thought it felt the size of a potato fork.

"Know how to use an ax, I see," he said. "You're close to the log, short like your pa." And then seeing a frown on my face, he added: "But I bet you grow up just as smart and with just as much music in you."

I figured that he knew I played the guitar good enough to second Dad on his fiddle at baptizings, funerals, and square dancing, which Mom didn't approve of, but knew we could use the money.

With his big hand still resting on my head, he looked over at Caleb.

"Still trading around, eh, Caleb?" he asked. "Sure you are. Too good at it to quit. Always good enough to get the better of old Apache every time."

12

I saw a frown on Caleb's face. But I didn't linger on that; I had troubles of my own. With Apache's big hand, rough as a cocklebur, still on my head, I was thinking about what Caleb had once told me about Apache's hands—how he could fold them like a leaf, slide either inside a hole narrow as a squint, and lift out a termite. Long, bony fingers pinching the nape of its neck firm but yet gentle as a doe rabbit carrying her young, gentle all the way to her nest—the nest, in Apache's case, being Echo Hollow. Up the hollow with the termite folded comfortable-like in the crook of his finger and lulled to sleep by the rock of his gait.

He squinted down at me, Indianish-like: "Never heard a hound bark when I drove up," he said, taking his hand off my head. "Mighty lonesome, a boy without a hound dog. Catch you a want that's powerful enough, and we maybe can work something out. Just hope you ain't learned too much about trading from Caleb."

He took the sack Weasel was holding and handed it to Caleb.

"Brought some wild honey over that Lottie sent to your ma," he said. "You can fetch it to her without taking her from her work." And then as Caleb turned to go, he said: "Ain't found me no widow women yet what's needing firewood, have you, Caleb?" He laughed into the wind.

Caleb was back out in time to hear the big truck churn out of hearing distance. I picked up the ax but my heart was not in splitting wood. It was beating with the excitement of a chance to get a hound dog from someone part-Indian. Any Indian in him at all, he'd know hound dogs! That would come natural with him. I could end up with something to brag on and also to take away the loneliness of the mountain, especially whenever Caleb was off loafing with older boys his own age.

I worried about it all so much that that night after we had gone to bed, I tried to pester something out of Caleb: "Know what Indian Apache is akin to?" I asked.

But Caleb never even ruffled the covers. He whispered back: "Sitting Bull."

"How come you know?" I asked, like I knew but he was not supposed to.

13

"Simple," Caleb said. "When it comes to being akin to something, no one picks a common. It's generally a king, queen, or a knight—if Indian: Sitting Bull. He was king of the mountain." I heard Caleb yawn. "Beats all! If all the people claiming kin to Sitting Bull was, he wouldn't have had time to do no fighting and making a name for himself; he'd been chasing and catching squaws all the time. Which is what I'd ruther been doing anyway." I felt Caleb pull the cover tighter around him.

"You figure it's Sitting Bull?" I asked.

"Tell you what," Caleb whispered. "Before you wake Mom and get us both in trouble, why don't I tell you how you can find out for sure whether he's akin to Sitting Bull or not?"

"How's that?" I asked, excited.

"You know Riff Souders," he said. "You've seen the old man down at Kelsey's before. You know where he lives. He's been on the mountain longer than anyone else and he'd know. He knows everything about the mountain. I always figured to ask him one day myself but never got around to it."

Knowing that Caleb was dropping off to sleep, I whispered: "Bet Apache knows hound dogs!"

"Stick to trapping," Caleb whispered back.

"Says you really know how to trade," I whispered.

"Nobody gets the better of Apache," Caleb said. "Go to sleep!"

4

At daybreak I was on my way over the mountain, picking my way through briars and underbrush and trying to make plans as to how I might ask Riff Souders about Apache. I knew so little about him firsthand. And didn't like to think about what I did know. I had seen him on occasion at Kelsey's but had only spoken to him once. I remembered that he was not the sort of man you could friendly-up with— cantankerous and always set to take the opposite of whatever was said to him. It had been that way with me. Trying to be friendly and show respect to an elder like Mom had taught me to do, I had simply said to him that it was a nice day outside. He swarped around with the hickory

14

cane he always carried and asked in front of everyone just how I knew whether it was a nice day or not when I was no bigger than a small turd. That brought a laugh from the old-timers and turned my face as red as the tail of a shoaling sucker-fish. Later, Kelsey May told me that Riff was like that unless you caught him just right.

I knew that he was beetle-like, wrinkled as a turtle, and that he lived alone in a two-room shack on the far side of the mountain. Too feeble with age to travel much, he depended on others to bring him grub once a week and medicine for his gout. The one who fetched him the grub and the medicine was Weasel. The grub he got at Kelsey's; the medicine, he claimed, was made from herbs and sent by Lottie. But mention of the gout medicine would bring grins from the old-timers at Kelsey's. But it brought no grin from Mom. She said it was a shame that Weasel took the old man a devil's brew when it was far past time the old man got right with his Maker.

On days that he felt like it, Riff grubbed a little along the mountain. But mostly he sat on his front porch trying to pull heat from the sun. I had seen him there times I was over that way squirreling, but because of what he had said to me at Kelsey's, I never stopped. But, looking down from high on the ridge, I could see his head bobbing from his thin neck like a sycamore ball caught in the wind. He always had a book in his lap although it was said that he couldn't read or write. It was also said that he never opened the book unless someone came and then he'd flip it open and go to jabbering like a jaybird like he was catching every word inside. Always the same book, worn and faded and with loose pages that he was forever tucking back inside the book's cover. He'd mark the book with a splint once company was there close enough. One thing about him remained the same: he was as changeable as the weather, running, generally, from bad to worse. A temper honed like blue steel. That not only would he take the opposite of what you said, but he had a way of pulling something out of you, especially boys. If you were a boy the penalty was generally the same: he'd catch you with a ball of ambeer chewed out of straight Kentucky burley and strong enough to kill bugs. If he had ever missed, a boy was not the target. His accuracy was a brag, straight as a rifle shot.

But, like Kelsey had said, if you caught him just right, the old man seemed pleased with your coming, asking questions, things about Sourwood Mountain. He took pride in what he knew, and also the fact that there was no one left old enough to dispute him, even if they had had nerve to do so. Catch him right, ask, and he'd generally leaf through the faded book like he was searching for the answer. He'd run his finger under a line that he would shield from sight if you looked. Too close and he'd pucker his lips. Warning enough! I remembered that Caleb had said to me before I left that I'd probably come out all right with the old man. Mainly because of what he had said to me that day at Kelsey's. That the old man was bad to worry and fret over something like that and tried to make amends.

What worried me now was something Earl Puckett had once told me. He had said that it was always better to stop at Riff Souder's right after Weasel had dropped off some medicine for his gout. That he seemed nervous and fretful without it. A bottle less than half full was the best time to stop, an empty bottle the worst. Trouble was, there was no way to know until you got there. Earl said he had caught him just right. That the old man had been happy enough to dance about, brittle-boned as he was. His little pipe-stemmed legs whirling in the air making popping noises like they were sure to break, but hadn't. Told Earl where to hunt and where to fish and that he'd been a general during the Civil War but not to tell anyone since they'd accuse him of bragging, and that on his trip over, he'd teach Earl how to spit. But, afraid his luck might run out, Earl hadn't gone back yet.

Knowing that my going there at best was as chancy as a summer rain, I was excited and miserable. I tried to think about the good side. If my luck held I might even learn how to spit. I would take up chewing when I was out of Mom's sight and ward off anything I wanted, like snakes and mosquitoes. I could find out about Apache and take back the answer I wanted. No one I knew would know the difference or ask. Riff's word was enough to settle, gospel-like when it dealt with Sourwood. He knew it all: the worst drought, the heaviest rains, the deepest snow, and the name of everyone buried in a sunken grave along the mountain with no marker.

The old man seemed to be in a happy mood when I reached his

place, and I thought that my luck had held. He seemed powerfully happy. He took a pull from the bottle of gout medicine and jumped to his pipe-stemmed legs and started to dance. I fairly expected his bones to pop. He grinned and tried to furnish his own music by whistling through withered lips as pale as a frosted persimmon. All that came out was wind and ambeer. He called me by name, which pleased me, and allowed as how if my dad was there with his fiddle, he'd show me a step or two. And then remembering that I seconded Dad on the guitar, he asked me to hum "Sourwood Mountain," and he'd do the best he could.

As I hummed, I glanced around to see if I could see the big hound, Fetchum, that Riff kept on the place, a hound that I had heard had been with Riff for so long that it was like him in many ways. Fetchum was particularly bad to side with Riff—moody and bad to go for your britches whenever Riff seemed put-out with you. I didn't see him and, judging from the looks of the old man, I wouldn't have long to search. He was drousying up. He mumbled about my coming back in a few days, and he'd furnish the tobacco and teach me how to spit. For me to think up anything I wanted to know about Sourwood Mountain, and he'd tell me. With time running out, I leaned toward him. But I was too late. His eyelids were closed, and he was snoring, asleep in his split-bottomed chair.

5

Afraid I might jinx my luck, I managed to keep secret what had happened during my visit to Riff Souders. Well, almost kept it. Caleb pestered me so much that I finally told him about the old man inviting me back over.

"That's a good sign," Caleb said. "Sounds like the old man is sure enough trying to make up for what he said to you down at Kelsey's place. I really ought to visit the old man myself; he's always been friendly with me."

A week later I crossed the mountain again, nervous and excited. I tried to temper my nervousness with thoughts of what all I might learn before high noon. About Apache and learning how to spit which would be a brag as long as I kept my distance from Mom; to her tobacco was akin to the devil.

But for some reason when I reached the old man's shack, I didn't think he seemed overpoweringly happy to see me. Nothing like I had hoped and dreamed it would be during the days I had waited. He was humped over in his chair trying to catch rays of sun. I saw his big hound Fetchum on the other end of the porch chewing on a root. The odor was so rank that I knew it was sassafras. The only thing moving on the old man were his jaws; he was chewing furious on his cud. Finally, with a neck that looked too small and wrinkled, he lifted his head and shot a spurt of ambeer into the yard.

"Didn't happen to see anything of Weasel on your way over, did you?" he grumbled.

"No," I answered, glad that the silence was broken.

He stared off up the path that led across the mountain. And sensing that things could get worse, I figured I'd better get Apache out of the way first and take a chance on being taught how to spit second. I asked him point-blank about Apache being part Indian. But instead of answering, he puckered his withered lips, spurted a wad of ambeer and caught me dead-center on the end of my big toe that I had stubbed a few days before. Made raw again by the stubble, underbrush, and wetness of the grass on my trip over, the ambeer burned like fire. Determined not to let that show, I just stood there acting like being hit on a raw toe with a wad of ambeer was a natural thing. He squinted at me. "No bigger than a fart and already a mister-know-it-all, eh?" he said. "Just like your brother, Caleb. Come strutting over here asking the same question, like he aimed to tell me what Apache is and ain't. Must run in the family, you figure?"

With the uneasy feeling that my own brother had just snuffed me out, I pondered my answer. I heard Fetchum growl but was afraid to look because I would have to take my eyes off the old man to do so, and I knew he was building another shot that might go anywhere. Slowly, I said: "I figure the same way you figure."

He didn't seem pleased by that at all.

"You little fart!" he said. "And now you're telling an old man what's

ciphered more books than you've had days on the mountain how he is
figuring!" And he set the end of my toe on fire again.

The big hound growled louder, and I glanced to see if he might be
slipping up on me. The old man had made our talk sound like an argu-
ment, and I knew the hound was ready to side with him—go for my
britches' leg as old as he was. Just how old no one knew. Marvin Yates
said that he had once heard the old man say he had gotten him during
the war. Trouble was he hadn't said which war. Marvin said that by the
looks of him it was probably the Civil War although that would have
made him mighty old. But he had been with Riff long enough to pick
up his ways. He eyed Riff to see how things set. I had me two worries
now: Riff and Fetchum.

"Got yourself just enough schooling over at Sourwood to make
you a mister-know-it-all, ain't you?" he asked. "Well, we'll see about
that once and for all mister uppity-know-it-all!"

The big hound dropped his sassafras root and stared at me with a
greater interest. And with one eye on Riff and one eye on the hound,
visions of my past started floating before me like I had heard they
would on the day of reckoning. I tried to figure a way to let the old
man know his word was gospel but was certain he'd object to that, too.
So, dazed, I never saw his cane coming, just felt the crook on the back
of my neck. The hound jumped to his feet, his hair hackled around his
neck. And this much I knew: a mistake now on my part, and you could
scratch me off forever! But then for some strange reason, I thought I
saw a smile cross his face. I caught a slender thread of hope when he
took his beady eyes off me and stared off up the mountain. I heard the
long tail of the big hound thumping the boards of the porch. The old
man backed the cane from my neck and visions of my past flittered
away. And then Riff raised a hand in welcome. I glanced and saw Weasel
coming toward the cabin.

"Got some more herb medicine Lottie sent over for your gout,"
Weasel said. And then hearing the drumming of the old hound's tail
Weasel looked toward him. "I'd stop that hound from chewing so much
sassafras, Riff. It'll thin his blood until he's too weak to walk."

"Not much I can do about it now," Riff answered. "He's took to sassafras like I've took to Lottie's tonic. Done learned to dig it for himself."

19

He pulled a long draw from the bottle Weasel handed him and blew hard, squinting his face. And then he burned my toe again with ambeer.

"Trying to heal this little nubbin's toe for him," he said. "Got it all rawed up coming to ask old Riff about things on Sourwood. I like to see that. Learn something, curious that way. Feel some responsible for his toe, though. Ambeer will do it; ain't nothing better on proud flesh."

"Ambeer is good," Weasel said. "But Lottie's got an herb cure. . . ." Hearing the growl come from the big hound, Weasel hesitated and then added: "that is a good second to ambeer."

And then the old man looked at me.

"Now about that question you asked . . . ," but his eyes trailed off. He watched Weasel casting about his weathered porch, fingering the cracks in the crooked poles that held the roof on. There was no way the old porch could hold against termites. And the old man was too old to catch a winter without a roof over his head. I heard the big hound growl. Termites, I thought, are not my problem now—to take leave and melt into the mountain was. I had my answer, and who was to know different? Just by being here was proof enough. And no boy with nerve enough to ask the old man the opposite.

On my way home, I circled by way of Sourwood Creek to wash the ambeer from my big toe. The water was cold, and I watched the minnows swim under the shadows of the limbs and then break into the sun, their bodies so frail that I could see through them. I watched a turtle make its way slowly through the current and end up at the mouth of a muskrat hole looking lonesome and sad in the clear water. I thought about being alone—without a hound dog. My want for one became almost unbearable. And sad myself, I looked forward to cold weather and trapping, especially the line I would run up Echo Hollow. How was I to know—Apache might have traded for a hound.

6

When the weather turned cold enough to prime furs, I worked my way up Echo Hollow. I planned to kill two birds with one stone; Echo Hollow should be one of the best places to trap for mink. The mountain was pocked with deserted coal mines that wormed under the mountain dark and deep. Mink, being one of the most curious of all varmints, and traveling by land as well as stream, would come up Echo to search the mines for mice that had gone inside the mines searching for warmth. The soft floors of the mines would hold tracks. And, also, being up Echo I could see if Apache had any hounds on his place.

I made a few sets within seeing distance of Apache's, high on the mountain next to a deserted coal tipple. Staring below I could see that Apache, or probably Lottie since she did most of the work around the cabin, had planted a long field of corn along the banks of Echo Creek, running in front of and away from the cabin. And knowing that this was the only field of corn along the creek, I knew that muskrats would gather there. The corn had been cut and shucked, and I knew that some of it would be used to grind into cornmeal and some left to feed the old mare mule. Some, also, would be drug to the creek by the muskrats. I decided to search for some trap sets there—close enough to the cabin to search, also, for a hound dog. If I got close enough for a hound to bark, that ought to please me and Lottie—Lottie that company might be coming, me that a hound was sure enough on the place. From high on the ridge, the brown shocks of corn looked like an Indian village below.

The steep banks of the creek hid me from sight of the cabin. I found several fresh muskrat slides and made sets there, setting my traps at the end of each slide just under the water and then covering them with water-soaked leaves from the bottom of the creek. Hearing no hound bark so far, I got curious enough to climb to the top of the steep bank and peep over; after all, there could have been a hound there that had run the mountain all night and was sleeping now.

Patting the grass down that grew on the rim of the bank, I peeped and saw Lottie hunkered in the yard, her long, woolen coat pulled around her. She hunkered in a thin beam of sun that had filtered through the trees and down the mountain. Trying to stretch for a better look, I knocked some of the loose dirt off with my foot, and it went tumbling into the water below. Hearing the noise, Lottie saw me. She beckoned, lured me with a long, lean finger. And with fear of her casting a spell on me, or giving up a chance to see a hound dog on the

21

place if I chose the opposite, I joined her there in the yard, the closest to her I had ever been.

"You cold?" she quivered, tucking the end of the woolen coat around her ankles.

Truth be, I was. Powerfully cold. I stood shivering but tried not to show it. My shoes were wet from making a mink set on Sourwood Creek. I had stepped into the water to leave no scent and scare a mink off, and I had gone in over the tops of my boots. Nothing would scare a mink away as fast as man-scent. Even the smell of a steel trap would do it, but I boiled my traps in walnut hulls to take the smell of steel away. With the bottoms of my britches wet and then frozen, my shuffling caused them to make a cracking noise.

"I had planned to build a fire on the mountain," I answered.

Lottie, hunkered down like an Indian squaw, studied that. The rim of the coat was soldered by the thin layer of ice that formed over the land. Her hair was rolled in a bun on the back of her head, and her face looked long and lean, her cheekbones tapered like a tomahawk. I thought she had the lonesomest eyes I had ever seen. The wind was up, and Lottie shivered. She pulled the long coat tighter around her. She looked off as if she was talking to the mountain. "Going now," she said. "The sun is. Giving way to snow clouds. Lord only knows when it will come again. Be a comfort and a blessing when it does, though." She searched the mountain with hollow eyes and then looked at me and grinned. Her teeth were worn, crooked, and stained. "Planning to build a fire, was you?"

"Planning," I answered, shifting about to warm my frozen feet.

She lifted her bony finger and pointed toward the top of the cabin and then let her finger follow the thin stream of smoke that drifted out of the chimney, rode the wind down the hollow like a ghost-garment.

"No need for you to build a fire when you can take heat from mine," she said. "Hot cup of sassafras tea will be like pouring sun down you. Whatever you are after will be there when you get back." She stared at the cold mountain. "Nothing much ever leaves this hollow except my menfolk. Lonesome. Well, hunker here beside me for a word of scripture. Pray for our shortcomings and being lean on the Word."

I did, coaxed by her lonesome eyes and the thought that on a morning such as this, no one would be on the mountain to see and tell. But it was a heavy price to pay for a cup of tea inside. Hunkered there, she exposed my ignorance on scripture and my want of worldly ways to both varmints and mountain. She gave thanks for the fire that would soon warm my hands and feet and for the tea that would warm my innards.

On our way to the cabin she asked about Mom and if she had used up the honey she had sent. She said she had had to leave more honey in the hives this year than usual for the bees to feed on since the signs told her it would be a hard winter. She said that living in Echo Hollow now, she seldom got to see her friends very often but prayed for them. She told me that she hoped Mom would take to coming to Slaboak Church and bringing me with her. She asked why I was on the mountain and creek, and when I told her I was trapping, she warned me to watch for her cat since he wandered off to the mines sometimes looking for mice. She leaned close and whispered: "Lord provides for them that prays."

I watched the words drift out of her mouth, slow and frost-white.

It was just this side of the porch while I was thinking that I'd probably be listening to scripture until the snow came knee-deep that my whole world changed! For standing near the end of the porch was the prettiest hound dog I had ever seen. He stared at me curious-like and then disappeared between two sandstone rocks that furnished the foundation for that end of the porch. Just that quick! Left me with a want more powerful than I had ever known. I caught Lottie staring at me and then looking at the small hole the hound had squeezed through.

"Quare hound," she said. "Quare and with sneaking ways. Apache took him in as boot on a termite job, he says. Claims he's a broken-down foxhound what's gone to treeing and says them makes the best tree-dogs. Slow and good on possum, Apache and Weasel says. But with no possum on the table, I ask the Lord's forgiveness for doubting. For doubting the ways of a hound and the word of men, especially when it comes to Apache and Weasel."

"They do make the best tree-dogs," I said, knowing that I had heard that said many times, but saying it in a voice that I hoped might coax the big hound back out from under the porch.

It didn't, and I followed Lottie inside the cabin to take heat from the potbellied stove that stood out in the room. Lottie turned up a coal-oil lamp and then ladled some hot water from a kettle she kept on top of the stove. She poured the hot water over some sassafras bark sliced off the root. Near the stove I noticed a bucket of water with a few ears of corn soaking in it. Corn, I thought, she was soaking for the old mule to eat.

I took heat from Lottie's stove and drank tea to scripture, swallowing on trials and tribulations. And, for shame, all the time thinking about the big hound under the porch. The hound as big in my mind as a mountain, scripture little enough to pass through the eye of a needle.

When I left, Lottie was standing in the yard holding a worn and faded Bible in her hand, the wind teasing the pages, opening, closing.

"You'll come visit again?" she asked. "The fire is never out this time of year."

I looked again into the lonesomest eyes I had ever seen.

"Yes," I said.

"I'm glad," she said. "Lonesome place, Echo Hollow."

And I walked back over the mountain lathered with scripture but thinking that it was a small price to pay for a look at the prettiest hound dog I had ever seen.

7

I went up Echo Hollow each day to check my traps and then join Lottie at the cabin. Not once had I seen Apache or Weasel there. Lottie told me they stayed late selling firewood. I wondered if Apache had located a parcel of widow women but didn't say anything to Lottie about that. I felt sad because she was alone all the time. I felt some shame too because of the reason I was there, mostly. I stole heat from her fire, drank her tea, and pretended to listen to scripture knowing that the real reason I was there was to try to catch another look at the hound, which I seldom got to do. The weather cold, he stayed mostly under the porch. Sometimes when I came up, I could see his rear-end sliding between the sandstone rocks. And I wondered how something that disappeared so quickly could leave so much behind to build dreams on. In time, I thought, he would friendly-up.

Excited one evening, I asked Lottie if she thought Apache would ever consider selling or trading the hound.

"Apache would most likely sell or trade anything that belonged to him," she answered, "even me! But I wouldn't be apt to fetch much, you know."

I had come to like Lottie. She was kind, gentle, and looked much prettier now than the first day I had come. I watched while her withered hands pushed a stick of wood inside the stove. Her skin looked so wrinkled and wind-cracked.

"You'd fetch a heap if I was trading," I said, almost without thinking. She cackled with laughter until the bun danced on the back of her head. She crooked her bony finger at me and said: "You a big'n for talk like that! But keep talking pretty-like, and it's apt to turn you a favor one day." And then she stared out the window. "Wouldn't do no good to ever trade for me. Nothing Apache has ever touched leaves him for good. A visit maybe, but always comes back."

But I could see that I had put a sparkle in her eyes, and I felt both good and ashamed. She walked that evening to the porch with me, carrying her Bible in her hand. I stood watching the old mare mule that she had named Maud wind her way off the slope and stop under the hackberry tree in the yard near the porch. She froze like a stump there and hung her head repenting-like. I figured she had probably come in for scripture. And I thought if there was ever a mule that had earned the Keys to the Kingdom it had to be her. If ever a mule walked right on through the Pearly Gates, I'd lay a bet her name was Maud. That is until I caught Lottie not looking and patted Maud on the nose out of sympathy, and she gummed my hand hard enough to hurt. I knew then she was as sorry as me. A hypocrite, the Keys to the Kingdom probably lost forever.

I walked up the mountain toward home remembering what Lottie had said about Apache: that he'd sell or trade anything he owned. As far as nothing ever leaving him for good, we'd see about that!

I turned once to wave at Lottie but saw that she wouldn't see. She stood at the edge of the porch with her Bible open reading, I knew, to the old mule. Old Maud and me had something in common: with Maud it was tolerating scripture for corn; with me it was tolerating scripture for the want of a hound dog.

8

A few days later the chance to bargain with Apache on the hound came. It was on a Sunday morning, and I had stepped into the mouth of Echo Hollow to check my traps. I was worried. There had been a heavy rain early Saturday night, and the creek had risen but had settled out by daylight. The water had been high enough to push brush on top of the banks and to carry some of it downstream lodging it in the bends. How many of the traps had been pulled out by the current and were inside the brushpiles, I didn't know.

Staring up the creek and wondering how many traps I might have lost, I saw Lottie floating out of a heavy mist and down the path that followed the creek toward me. Being Sunday morning I knew that she was on her way to Slaboak Church. I knew that she'd be thinking that that was where I ought to be, too. There was no time to hide if I had wanted to. Floating in front of me, she stopped for a moment. She spoke of the heavy rain that had come but that the good Lord had settled so she could make it to church, and I told her that I was afraid I had lost some traps. Hunkering me with her bony finger, she prayed that I might come to know that losing a trap was better than losing a soul. She rose slowly, and I heard her bones squeak. She tucked her Bible inside her coat to protect it from the dampness. And then she looked down at me and said: "Last night was a time for losing. I lost another of my hens, red-combed and laying. Found her feathers outside the hole under the porch that that hound goes through to hide-out. I told Apache about my suspicions." Her eyes looked fiery.

"I'd say this morning would be a good time to talk with him about a trade on a hound dog if you stop that way. He was along the creek

26

gathering driftwood for the stove when I left. Does things like that when he's trying to get back on the good-side."

Bending her bony finger and pecking it at me, I knew it was time for me to hunker again. I did, feeling some akin to old Maud. This time she prayed that I'd be forgiven for bargaining on Sunday if I did run into Apache. The Lord's day! But, for shame, I thought only of the hound dog.

I did a lot of thinking between the mouth of the creek and the front of Apache's cabin. Lottie's loss could be my gain! And what Apache had caught from her would make him ripe. That the hound might have stolen a chicken meant little to me. To break a hound of that was easy. All you had to do was tie a dead chicken around his neck and make him carry it until he thought it belonged there and then he'd stop. I'd break him of that before Mom had to worry about the chickens she kept at our house.

Close enough to the cabin to be seen, and set on making enough noise to be heard, I busied myself inside a brushpile, threw the limbs that I broke loose high on the bank. I didn't have to wait long. Through the tangled limbs of the brushpile, I saw him staring down at me. Wisps of fog were settled on his beard heavy enough to bead, and he shook it off like a dog shaking water from its coat. He looked as large as a giant. I pulled at the brush and said: "Washout is bad for trapping."

"But good if you're gathering brushwood," he answered. He laughed into the wind. "Any luck on catching varmints?"

"Catching a few muskrats and a possum now and then," I answered. "But I'm hoping for mink, mostly." He laughed again.

"Could have your sights set a mite too high," he said. "Mink is hard to out-smart. What you been doing with the carcasses of the muskrats and possums?"

"Some I sell to the shantyboat people over on the river," I said.

"Good eating, muskrats," he said. "Lottie takes to possum. Ain't nothing that sweetens her like a fat possum. I might have a mind to buy some carcasses from you if they ain't been out of the trap too long or winter-poor. Might buy or bargain."

And remembering what Lottie had said, I caught my breath. I even thought of her last prayer. But I figured I'd try to bargain for the hound first and hope to shuck my sin for doing so later.

"I'd bargain on as many as you'd be wanting," I said.

Apache screwed up a patch of his beard and grinned. He said: "I don't know about trying to bargain with you. You could be like your brother Caleb and clean shuck me out. What ever could you be wanting to shuck me out of anyway?"

"A hound dog, mostly," I answered.

Apache stared off like he was studying, and I got to thinking that I might have come to the heart of the trade too quickly. In trading, Caleb had told me, you ought to start off by striking fault on whatever you're trading for. Apache frowned.

"I know you got your sights set a mite high," he said. He pondered that. "But it's natural, I guess. A boy and a hound. Trouble is, I ain't got but one hound on the place, and Lottie has done took a powerful liking to him. I trade old Sneakin off, and she's apt to skin me!"

"Sneakin!" I said, hoping what was crossing my mind was not so.

"Name he brought with him" Apache said. "Lottie kept to it. Powerful dog to sneak up on game. He's gooder then good'n! He comes to it."

Knowing that Lottie had probably named him, my heart sunk. Good golly, I thought, why did she have to go sticking a name like that on a hound so pretty? But I thought I knew. I knew also that an owner had a right to name a dog whatever he wanted, but also figured that a new owner had a right to change it just as quickly.

"Trade on him?" I asked.

"You're set higher than mink, boy," Apache answered. "Some hounds are traders, and some hounds are keepers; Sneakin is a keeper!" He stared off over the mountain and shook his head. "But trading is a fever with me. I'm apt to sell or trade anything that belongs to me if the price is right. I lose more good hounds that way. Lost old Geronimo because of the fever a while back."

With a head full of hound dog, I hurried: "What you figuring to trade to?"

Apache stared down at me.

28

"See you're good about getting in and out of small places," he said. "But, no; I got Weasel for that. I just wished I wasn't seeing the lonely in your eyes I been seeing in the eyes of that hound. Me being gone most of the time, he's got to hunt alone. There's just something betwixt a boy and a hound that ain't betwixt a man and hound. Tell you what: you be willing to bring them carcasses by the cabin this winter and do a little work for me termiting when the weather breaks, and you've done traded me out of the best tree dog I ever owned." He reached down and pinched me on the shoulder. He grinned. "When it comes to trading, you got Caleb beat from here to the river. Fetch the hound home after you have lived up to your end of the bargain. Come visit with him all you want until you have. Gives me time to settle with Lottie."

And the trade was sealed then and there. I left the hollow feeling not one bit sorry that I had just skinned Apache out. I thought mostly of the name I would give the big hound. A name that would fetch a brag: Thunder, Bugle, or the sort. For I knew that he would have a voice that would tremble the mountain.

But in the days that followed, I found out that trading for the hound was not going to be as easy as I had thought. I even thought that Caleb might be right: that nothing was fast and easy with Apache attached to it. I carried carcasses until I lost count. Apache pushed me to the edge of give-up but always brought me back with hound dog brag. And the thing was, the hound offered little help. He was still as shy as a fox. Somehow I knew that Lottie knew, although she never asked. But she read scripture to me faster and more furious. Maybe preparing me for something that might happen later on. But I stayed with my bargain and fought the winter through.

With the coming of warm weather, I went to work on the termite truck. Mom was not too pleased. She worried that I might get hurt or pick up bad habits from Apache and Weasel. But, thinking I was proud of my first job, she agreed to tolerate until she had more time to judge. I figured Caleb was glad to have more time loafing with boys his own age and not having me around to pester so much.

I started out each morning riding on the bed of the truck with

Weasel. Apache, comfortable-like, did all the driving. Weasel, his long hair blowing in the wind like the mane of a horse was lucky, I thought— lucky that he had lost his power of smell. The odor took my breath away, but worse were the flies. They were as thick around the tanks as swarms of bees and made my life miserable. They bit me, crawled up my britches until I tied the bottom of the legs off, and crawled over my eyelids. I kept my mouth closed. One evening just before quitting time a fly or something crawled down inside my ear and hummed like a motor. I thought it would drive me crazy. Catching Caleb off where Mom couldn't hear, I told him about it.

"Probably a fly or baby termite," he said, coaxing me up the side of the mountain. He blew tobacco smoke down my ear and stopped the motor in a hurry.

The smoke from my ear and hair almost cost me my job. Mom scented it and asked me if Apache or Weasel was trying to teach me how to smoke. I told her the smoke must have come from Weasel's pipe, and that seemed to settle it even though he didn't smoke.

The flies that pestered me were fair game to both Apache and Weasel. Both chewed on the job and were able to spit just this side of Riff Souder. They tried to pick flies off like quail on the wing. Trouble was, a hit or a miss generally left me looking like I had a face full of freckles. Whenever I came close to quitting, Apache would invite me to ride in the truck with him. But, all-in-all, that turned me little favor. For one thing Weasel pouted because of it and worked me harder. For another, Apache kept both windows cracked because of the fumes from the truck, and the flies came in one window and rode the wind out the other. On their way across, Apache shot at them with birdshots of ambeer. The ones he hit fell on me and, unable to fly, they crawled, which made it worse. When we got on the job, I paid for the cab ride, especially under the houses. I slid under the joist, dragged the hose, did the spraying and caught all the smell. Weasel would crawl off and eat a raw turnip, reminding me that the grinding I heard was him and not a termite since a termite ate society-like, silent, same as the uppities in Sourwood.

I went home of the evening smelling so bad that Mom made me either drop first at the rain barrel or the creek. And when Caleb complained that I smelled too bad to sleep with, she threw in a bar of lye soap.

Days were so long. "Just a little longer," Apache would coax, "and the hound is yours."

For the love of a hound dog, I stuck it out. One evening Apache said to me: "You can fetch your hound whenever you want."

9

It had just broken daylight when I stepped inside the mouth of Echo Hollow. With my want so close, the whole Hollow seemed to change. It no longer seemed dark and dreary. The fog that hovered like a sitting hen looked soft and pretty, and I stopped for a moment to listen to it drip, dripping from the limbs of the trees. Redbirds burst from everywhere like puffs of fire. Moss under my feet melted to my ankles. Echo Creek churned over rocks milk-white and pooled blue as a robin's egg. I hummed with the birds, wind, and creek; a pretty song.

Lottie met me in the yard and told me Apache and Weasel were in the outbuilding where they kept supplies. But Apache must have heard our talking. I watched the door to the outbuilding open, and he ducked under the door-frame.

"Come early," he said, rubbing his beard. "Well, one more thing to do, and he's yours."

I thought my heart would stop.

"You'll have to get him out from under the porch," he said. "Probably hating to leave."

I didn't figure fetching the big hound from under the porch would be much of a problem. I had had the summer to practice getting in and out of tight places, and searching for something as big as a hound dog was a heap-sight easier than something as little as a termite.

I wormed my way between the sandstone rocks and then squeezed to get under the joist that held the porch floor, a floor so low to the earth that in places I had to scoop dirt out to get under. I couldn't help but noticing doodles of sawdust and tunnels in the joist, all signs of termites. I thought of what I had heard Mom say about Dad: being a shoe cobbler and his own family the only ones in Sourwood who needed their shoes fixed.

31

I found the big hound hunkered near the far side of the porch. He eyed me with suspicion but pleased me by thumping the dust with his tail. I slipped a rope around his neck and coaxed.

"Let's go home, Thunder," I said, naming him on the spot.

He didn't come, and I ended up having to shove him out ahead of me. Lottie, her Bible in her hand, stood outside the hole waiting for us.

"You sure it's all right with your ma for you to have that hound?" she asked.

"Yes," I answered, since I had told Mom that I might get me a dog but that my summer wages would not be going for it. I had kept money back from the sale of varmint hides to cover my lie, money that Mom hoped I would use toward schooling.

"Well," Lottie said, "we better have a little scripture for the ways of a hound and the want of a boy."

And while she prayed and told of the misgivings of both, I prayed for shortness. The big hound, restless, pulled at the rope. But Lottie stomped her foot, and the hound dropped its head repenting-like, just like old Maud.

When we reached the edge of the yard, she waved her hand and said: "Have a nice visit."

And for some reason I thought she might not be talking to me. But with a hound on the end of my rope, I didn't dwell on that.

10

Mom never made much fuss over the hound at all; like a hound was something for her to tolerate with boys on the place. She did squint down at him with her hands on her hips and warn me about watching him around her chickens. I never figured that meant Lottie had said anything—Mom had long ago learned the ways of some dogs. My problem was not chickens; it was getting the hound used to his new name.

"That's the trouble with old dogs what's already had a name tacked on them," Caleb said. "Sometimes you can tack a new name on one and sometimes never."

"How long you think it might take?" I asked, knowing what would happen if word of his old name got out.

"Hard to tell," Caleb said. "But I'd ease the new name on him. Like when you go swimming, and the creek is cold. You stick a toe in and let the cold creep up. Next thing you know, you're swimming around independent-like. Give the dog time."

Caleb had gotten himself a job working in the corn bottoms along Sourwood Creek for Elias Skaggs. It was a long field, and Caleb's job was to shuck half the field, leave the ear on the other half, and when that was finished, he was to put the field up in shocks. The pay was not that high, but the job was steady, and Elias was never there to bother you. When the field of corn was finished, Elias said he'd probably have some more work, especially on weekends, up at the barn on his place where they fought game chickens. If I wanted, Caleb said, he could probably get me on at both places. Give me a chance to earn some trap money and learn something to boot.

But I chose to stay with Thunder. I was desperate enough to try anything on him. I called him Sneakin whenever I thought he was too far away from me and eased Thunder on him when he was close enough to snuggle up to. I figured my time was short; Caleb would not keep a secret for long.

Reaching a low ebb, I tried to tack favors on the hound. He did have looks. His red and white coat marked him for a pure Walker, the best foxhounds of the lot. His ears were long and held no slits from either varmint or fence. His chest was deep enough to hold wind, and while I did not like the word "broken-down," old timers did claim that a broken-down foxhound—one that had stopped running fox—did make the greatest of tree dogs. That Apache said Sneakin had settled on possum pleased me. Coon would take him too far away, and a red fox would run all night and all the way to Kingdom Come. I didn't want a foxhound that ran fox. I didn't want to sit on a lonely ridge with old men all night where the voice of the hound was greater than the game he caught. Foxhounds never caught the fox. They simply ran him until their voices became whispers. Tired and stiff, they dropped off anywhere on the mountain to sleep. That could be miles away. Foxhunters spent as much time searching for their hounds as they did hunting them. I wanted a hound that would be around when I needed him, which was all the time.

When it came to the voice of the big hound, he was second to none. He could tremble the mountain, matching the name I had tried to give him. Trouble was, there was never anything that I could find on the end of it. I searched trees until my neck was stiff, the big hound excited and chewing the trunk of the tree like he was trying to drop the tree and get at the varmint; I dug inside holes until my fingers were raw, the big hound scratching and digging furious. We caught nothing.

Tired and brokenhearted, doubt crept in. I became curious and suspicious: like Lottie telling me once that nothing Apache ever touched was left natural; like whenever I scolded him, he dropped his head repenting-like, same as old Maud. And, worse, I could still see her bony finger and hear her call after us that nothing ever left Apache for good—for the hound to have a nice visit. I had visions of the big hound sneaking back to Apache's. I had started tying him at night after we had come off the mountain, using a rope with enough slack for him to crawl under Mom's porch where he slept.

I built a doghouse so that he would stop sleeping under the porch, which caused Mom to fuss because she knew that the big dog was carrying fleas there. It was disappointing. I had used some of the money I was saving for traps to buy boards and nails, and he never slept a night inside it. He still favored under Mom's porch. Seeing me struggle to get him out, Mom tacked a favor on him now and then. Mom was like that.

And then one night just when things looked the bleakest, a strange thing happened that was to change the lives of both me and that hound. It happened because of a want and a mix-up.

11

The greatest foxhound to ever run a trail on Sourwood Mountain had belonged to an old hermit who lived off a spur-hollow up Nebo. Tales of the big hound were always being told around foxfires and down at Kelsey's whenever talk got around to hound dogs. With old-timers there whittling, the talk was generally on foxhounds, and tales of a big hound that could unravel a scent from a hard frost. After the old man had died some time back, the hound had disappeared. He had not been seen or heard for some time now.

Woodrow Marson was a hermit all his life. He had grubbed a garden on a slope so steep that old men at Kelsey's said he planted with a shotgun, but mostly he gathered herbs off the mountain and sold them in Sourwood, trading some on occasion to Kelsey for grub. The big hound always stayed behind to watch the place when the old man was gone, and it was said that they ate at the same table and slept in the same bed. One thing was certain: he furnished the sweetest music this side of Gabriel.

As foxhunting went, the big hound had but one flaw: he was a loner like Woodrow and would not run with a pack which made him a devil to break up a chase. He'd strike the trail ahead of the other hounds and run the fox to Kingdom Come. And while foxhunters cursed him for that, they settled back and listened to his sweet music—a deep bugle voice that trembled the mountain, a song that lingered with them long after the chase was over. Knowing that the old man would never sell the hound, they offered good money for Woodrow to let him stand at stud. But for whatever reason, Woodrow chose to let him die with his music in him.

I could just remember the old man and Mom buying herbs from him on occasion. I remembered that Mom had gone to his funeral because she thought there would be hardly anyone there and that no one should go to his grave without someone to mourn. He had died off on the mountain searching for herbs and had been found by hunters days later.

After word of his passing spread, foxhunters figured that a hound with no owner was fair game. Some who had gone to the funeral had seen the big hound standing alone on the ridge above, but he never came to the grave site, stood like a ghost, coming to no call. And when some tried to coax and get closer, he melted into the mountain.

Foxhunters wasted no time returning to the shack where the old man had lived. They staked it out both day and night, but the hound never came. Some feared that he had left the mountain for good. And then one night they heard him ahead of their pack. Knowing that he was still on the mountain, probably hungry, they baited for him, but the food either became stale or was eaten by varmints. Next, they took bitch dogs in heat and staked them out near the shack, but the bitch dogs either ended up barren or whelped curs.

The big hound had only been seen once more, this time by a squirrel hunter. The hunter had been waiting on a ridge at the break of day for squirrels to cross over to a shellbark hickory that they had been cutting in the day before. He heard the mournful wail of a hound and peeped down the slope. He saw the big hound standing over Woodrow Marson's grave, his head high and wailing sorrowful enough to have nightmares attached to it. He watched the hound stretch out over the grave and rest there. It was so pitiful that he hadn't had the heart to bother him.

With recollections that some dogs would die of grief for their masters, some thought the big hound might have done just that, his bones scattered over half of Sourwood Mountain by buzzards.

The want and the mix-up happened one night when I had gone on the mountain with Sneakin to hunt, and we had wandered upon some foxhunters building a foxfire along the ridge. Sneakin, skittish around almost anyone except me, hid off in the bushes. He thought he had hid off, but two of the foxhunters saw him. With size and markings, he was a spitting image of the Woodrow Marson foxhound. They eased up to take a better look, and Sneakin melted into the mountain—a habit belonging to the Woodrow Marson foxhound. They inquired as to how I had come about the hound. Remembering that Lottie had said nothing ever leaves Apache for good, and with fear that the big hound might one day slip back off over there and that Apache might trade him off before I could fetch him, I lied. I told them that I had found him along the mountain. That was just what they wanted to hear, and just like Mom had said, that one lie makes another lie a certain. I told them that I had found him rib-poor. From there everything fit: the big hound had come to the want of a boy. It had happened before.

To make matters worse, Sneakin had wandered off down the mountain, hit a trail, and opened up. His deep, bugle voice trembled the moun-

36

tain, and that night by the dancing flames of a foxfire, I learned that a want could whip the truth backwards and slaunch-wise. Then and there Sneakin became the Woodrow Marson foxhound, and nothing I could do or say during the days that followed could ever change that.

During the days that followed, what they couldn't get from me they got from Caleb. I had made the mistake of telling him about the night on the mountain. Without saying anything to me, he tacked it on. He told them that the big hound had come from over on Durbin. He told them that Apache had taken the hound in on a termite job for an ailing widow lady whom he had heard Mom say she thought was a half-sister to Woodrow Marson and probably dead by now. He told them I had lied about the hound because I was afraid I would lose him. He recalled that Mom had said she thought the old woman had visited Woodrow on occasion before she had become too sick to make the trip. With the bait out he never had to say more. It all fit. The Marson hound had made up with her on her trips to the shack and had followed her home one day when she had come after some of the old man's plunder.

While Caleb spread rumors, I had troubles of my own. Mainly, Sneakin had started sneaking off, just as I had feared. The first day he had disappeared, I had called along the mountain until my voice became a whisper, and then remembering again Lottie's words, I went to Apache's and found him there sure enough. Scooting him again out from under the porch, Lottie stood waiting.

"Visit over!" she scolded.

The big hound drooped his head repenting-like.

Maybe seeing how the big hound had filled out she said: "I hope it ain't chickens what's pooched you out."

After scripture I took him home.

Two days later he was gone again. I found him again at Apache's. This time his sneaking off cost him a scolding and me the story of Moses.

When he disappeared again, and I went to Apache's to get him, I saw a man out in the yard talking to Lottie. My heart sank. Thinking that they hadn't seen me coming yet, I hid off in the bushes but close enough to hear.

"Just happened to be close," he said. "Thought I might stop to see if Apache might have a mind to trade back that old broken-down hound he got from me a while back as boot on a termite job. Didn't figure at the time I was as attached to that hound as I ended up being. And my woman is complaining that there ain't no dog around now to fight snakes."

"Peculiar," she answered. "Been a passel of menfolk up here lately inquiring about that hound. Be something if they'd come inquiring about scripture that way. Well, hard to catch Apache or Weasel here. Either termiting or selling firewood or trading." She looked off over the yard, and I was certain that she saw me. "Wouldn't be apt to do you any good if he was here, though. That hound wandered off a while back, and we done give up on him." She frowned as she watched the man spurt ambeer in her yard, and I knew that that would cost him. "If he was to wander back, there'd be no trading, though. I've done took a liking to that hound myself." Lottie stared again toward me. "Get shed of your termites?"

"Hard to tell," he answered. "Weeds growing so rank all along the foundation. But, won't matter long. I'm too old to be grubbing weeds, and the old woman's afraid of snakes. We're planning to move to Elliot County. Kin left the little woman a strip of land over there that's got enough coal on it to bring in a little money and furnish winter heat."

"Far piece," Lottie said.

"Used to raise hogs on it so they ain't apt to be many snakes," he said. He turned to go, but Lottie touched his arm.

"Stay for scripture," she said. "Pray for your having a place to move to and that your woman don't get bit by snakes."

After he had paid for the ambeer, Lottie motioned me in.

"I'd take that hound back by way of the mountain," she said. She shook her head and the bun danced like a sycamore ball. "Land sakes! What could be bringing all them menfolk up here inquiring about that useless hound!"

I shuffled my feet in the dust and looked down. I felt her bony hand lift my chin.

"Ain't useless to a boy though, is he," she said. "Old women are bad to get their tongues twisted at times. But I ain't said nothing about all the menfolk coming up here asking about the hound to either Apache or Weasel. I can't promise he won't find out on his own, though."

She bent over and hugged my neck, and I felt her tears on my face. "You best be going," she said.

And I picked my way up the mountain, leading the hound with a rope. I looked down at him; as sorry as I knew he was, he was all that I had. I had built too many dreams to lose him unless I had to. Near the top of the ridge, I stopped and looked back to the cabin. I could see Lottie still standing in the yard. She looked no taller than my finger was long. I thought of the lie she had told, maybe the first one she had ever told. I crossed the mountain with guilt almost unbearable.

This side of the house I saw Caleb standing in the yard. He had been talking to a man who had turned to walk off. I waited until he was out of sight and made my way in.

"Who was that?" I asked.

"Look," he said, "that dog can make us both rich. He ain't going to stay home anyway."

Knowing that Caleb knew that I knew, I answered: "I can tell them he ain't the Woodrow Marson foxhound," I said.

"They won't believe you," Caleb answered. "The more you deny the more they'll believe. They want him to be and that makes all the difference."

"How come?" I asked.

"I don't know," Caleb answered. "Maybe it's the same as you and me wanting something to be. They'll just figure you're holding out for a higher price. We could make some good money right now. He's going to end up at Apache's, and Apache'll get the money."

"But I love the old hound," I said.

"That's the trouble," Caleb said. "Love always getting in the way of common sense—is with me on girls and you on a hound dog."

Several days later, after Sneakin had disappeared, and I had gone to Lottie's to fetch him, I saw her standing in the yard with her Bible. I could tell by her look that something was wrong. She hugged my neck when I walked up and whispered in my ear: "The Lord giveth, and the Lord taketh away; blessed be the name of the Lord."

I knew then that Apache had found out and had traded him off. I knew, also, that I too had been spun in Apache's web—cocoon-tight!

But as I left the hollow that day, I was also remembering something else that I heard Lottie say among her scripture about the Lord helping them that helped themselves, and being all downcast wasn't about to help anything. I had been around Lottie long enough to know that there was no right in asking a great man like that Lord to help me get a little thing like a hound dog with all the other work He had to do, but it was good to know that He wouldn't be working against me either. I just needed to help myself. And I figured to do that: help myself right into a good hound dog.

To begin with, I needed to be more careful this time—not end up with a hound that spent all his time going from one place to the other, a hound that couldn't make up his mind or had a spell cast on him by someone like Apache. Not one that caused you to toss in bed all night wondering if he'd be there when daylight came, or made your heart skip every time he slipped inside the woods wondering if he would come back out the way he went in.

One thing was for certain: I had spent the better part of spring working for Apache and Weasel and traveling back and forth looking for that hound. Caleb said that I had spent enough time up there going after that dog alone for Lottie to scripture me up to gospel but wouldn't do no good because I was a hypocrite.

"How's that?" I asked

"Simple," Caleb answered, "you're going for the dog instead of scripture. You'll have to pay for all that one day, you know; listening to words of gospel with only hound dog on your mind."

Caleb also said that I had pestered him so much that he was just this side of being turned against hound dogs completely, but he said nothing about how he pestered me even more about this girl or that girl down at Sourwood School or at Slaboak Church. Truth was, he had gone for girls like I had gone for dogs and claimed that dogs were nothing more than crossover to the other, and that I'd find out one day after I got old enough to know the difference.

But when it came to speaking of differences between the two, I had heard some of the old men who sat Saturdays at Kelsey May's

General Store, whittling and knife-trading, say there generally wasn't a shaving difference betwixt the two: both were pretty, had a sweet mouth that seldom stopped, and traipsed after you until they got you treed. But, all in all, they claimed the longer shaving probably belonged to the hound being that they were the easier of the two to get shed of—as if you'd want to ever get shed of a hound dog, I thought.

I also thought of another difference, too: you didn't have to spend money to take a hound to a picture show like Caleb had to with girls, and a hound would settle for a leftover bone instead of a sack of popcorn that Caleb had to buy for a girl before she would watch the show with him.

But Caleb said that the picture show wasn't just all girls, especially when another boy had beat him out, but it was a way of seeing and knowing there was life and things outside of Sourwood, and often I joined him there when he had to go alone. And whenever we had enough money between us, we'd share a sack of popcorn. I liked being with Caleb; it was next to being on the mountain.

But, like I say, I had set my sights that day for a hound dog that would stay put. I had served my time in Apache and Weasel's web along with all the other boys before me, just like Caleb said I would end up doing.

Once out of the hollow that day, I had made the most of what was left of the summer without seeing either of them. I did see Lottie on occasion in Sourwood. She'd always crook me over with her lean and cold finger and lay enough scripture on me to guide me until we met again while I hunkered up into nothing that I hoped any of the boys could see, pass on, and tease me about.

She never spoke of a dog or either Apache or Weasel. But I often thought as I watched her turn and walk off, her long coat tucked tight and the edges touching the earth, how I wished she was as shed of Apache and Weasel as I was—or thought I was. Little did I know that I had one more stand to go before I was completely free and that the last wiggle out would be apt to follow me like a birthmark.

It had its beginning not long after I had hooked me a job down at Kelsey May's General Store afternoons after school and Saturdays when everyone along the mountain came to town to shop. Mom didn't cut

41

much fuss the day I told her about the job but just cautioned me that there was more to the mountains than hound dogs and what money I earned ought to go toward my schooling.

Mom had mentioned hound dogs when I told her about the job at Kelsey's because she knew that Kelsey was first and foremost a hound dog man. I mean, he had dogs around his place like a man ought to have dogs, which set well with me but caused Mom to remind me that in the mountains, a hound dog man and fiddle player had one thing mostly in common: a wanderer's foot. For both it was generally traipsing off nights when they ought to be home looking after their families.

That Mom felt the way she did about hounds and hound dog men made it hard for me. I mean, being around the house with a dream busting at the seams and no one to tell it to. No fiddles, just hound dogs. I planned to own me a parcel like Kelsey one day and spend my life off on Sourwood Mountain hunting.

Kelsey's store stood just about the center of town where the road made a stiff bend to pick up the more level land along the river. Mostly my job was to carry all sorts of feed and merchandise out of the store early of the mornings before school and on Saturdays and set it up to coax passersby to buy. Just this side of dark, I carried it back inside to keep them from stealing it.

Sometimes Kelsey would let me stock the shelves and now and then wait on a customer if he was off talking to a customer—always about a hound dog, I hoped. Waiting on customers, I got to open the big cash register, and it gave me something to build a dream on, seeing all the greenbacks in there. A dream of being rich one day myself, probably hunting in foreign lands and running a trapline all the way to Alaska whenever I wasn't laying off on some island somewhere under a tree to dodge the hot sun, sipping a sody pop. I mean, islands like you could find in some of the books down at Sourwood School. Me on an island, just sipping away, and with at least two hounds at my two sides. Caleb said that I might run into him sometimes on one of the islands where he'd be sipping a sody pop also but with two pretty girls at his two sides instead of hounds. As for Alaska, I'd just have to get used to being without him. Alaska was colder than Echo Hollow, and all the girls there were too fat from eating blubber and had to be pulled around on sleds all the time while you risked your life trying to get enough bear skins to keep them warm. Bear skins were all they wore.

"How do you know something like that?" I asked him once.

"Simply because if it has anything to do with a girl, I know it all," he answered.

I let it go at that because I figured by the time I was Caleb's age, it would be the same way with me when it came to hound dogs. I was already far ahead of him when it came to hunting and shooting.

But even greater than seeing the inside of the cash register was that sometimes I would get to see and hear Kelsey strike a trade in the blink of an eye for a coon, possum, or groundhog dog, but fairly empty a shelf of merchandise for a good squirrel dog. Good squirrel dogs were the hardest of all to come by, and that's what it took to pinch Kelsey's poke.

Most of his trades for dogs came from people up the Big Sandy River, all the way from the breaks at Elkhorn City on down. And most of the ones who came to trade had one thing in common: they were short on money but heavy on dogs, either their own or their neighbor's, as Kelsey had found out on more than one occasion. Any dog that wandered too far from home was asking for a trip, Caleb said. But, let that be—what pleased me about the whole thing was that Kelsey never turned down a trade. No matter their size, Kelsey figured every dog was worth at least one try on the mountain. That way you could see what was under the hair and hide.

And so it was one evening while I was working inside the store, I squinted and saw Weasel walk in, crook Kelsey to the side with his finger. Then I heard him bragging on a little feist that he and Apache had traded for on a termite job at a preacher's house along the Midland Trail. The dog was named Beanbug, and the preacher had cried when he let her go but said that his woman had passed away six months past, and he had had to take to circuit riding. Whenever she wasn't out treeing squirrels, the little Beanbug feist was listening to scripture. Hard to tell which she liked the most. She had been raised right.

"Don't let the name fool you," Weasel coaxed. "What this little dog don't know about putting a squirrel up a tree would slide through the eye of a needle. Raised by a gospel man, she came as a Godsend to Lottie who went right on scripturing her up until her sides pooched out!"

"What's the gospel got to do with hunting?" Kelsey said, liking a drink now and then but lean on scripture according to Mom.

"I'll tell you what it means," Weasel said. "It means like the scripture says you oughten, she won't tell a lie. She barks treed, grease the skillet!"

While Kelsey rubbed his chin and cast his eyes across the shelves of merchandise, probably wondering, I thought, what Weasel might be apt to strike a trade on. I couldn't stop myself from staring at Weasel myself. I mean, even with all the times I had been around him, I still wondered how so much talk could be packed inside so small a frame. Generally, I had not wanted to take much of it in, but being on hunting dogs today I wanted it all and more. And while I stared and waited, I couldn't help but remember what Mom had said once when I had asked her how so many words could be packed inside so small a man. She had said: "The wonder is that he can pack so many and not a thread of truth to a single one!"

Well, brag-talk led from one thing to another but ended up with plans for a squirrel hunt over on Nebo Ridge where the red squirrels had gone to cutting heavy on a grove of shagbark hickories. The hunt would include Kelsey's brother-in-law Pos Bailey, Pos's brother Leifford, Weasel, Beanbug, and me—Weasel figuring me to be handy to carry the kill, shaming me in front of Kelsey since I figured I was about as good at squirrel hunting as anyone on Sourwood Mountain, no matter the age.

The night before the morning of the hunt, I cleaned the big mule-eared double-barrel twelve that Dad let me use, grew restless trying to figure how and when I could sell all the squirrels I'd be bringing back if the Beanbug dog was even close to what Weasel said she was. I had never known a dog that wouldn't lie, but then, I'd never known a dog that was all gospeled-up. Could be that Kelsey would be so happy about getting to own a dog like Beanbug that he'd let me gut the squirrels and hang them for sale on a hook outside his store. That way I could try a little selling and bragging at the same time.

On our way over to Nebo, Weasel never stopped bragging about the little feist. How most of the time, outside of going off to hunt squirrels, had been spent on the little cabin porch listening while Lottie read scripture, scripture that took, especially when it came to lying. Lie in front of her, and she'd tuck her tail betwixt her hind legs, roll over on her back like she was waiting for judgment to come! An oath would put her this side of the Pearly Gates, and taking the Lord's name in vain might unlock the Gate, ending the hunt. So we needed to be careful of our talk, which didn't bother me since I didn't cuss anyway except now and then when I was out of Mom's hearing.

I'll say this about the Beanbug dog: she was named right, even if it was a name I'd find hard to live with on a dog I owned. She was more spotted than any dog I had ever seen. She looked exactly like a beanbug! And so small and low to the ground that she could have been mistaken for a squirrel if the colors had matched, but I figured you couldn't tell a dog by its looks.

She seemed frisky when we turned her into the woods, which brought an "I told you so" look from Weasel and pleased us all. And she kept out of our way, but by walking behind us up the path to the ridge when it seemed to me she ought to be up ahead like a squirrel dog, out winding for scent and knocking the morning dew off the weeds hanging over the path, getting her wet instead of us. I mean, I noticed things like that. Kelsey did, too—which caused Weasel to pull up.

"Give her room!" he said to me, as if I was the only one on the path with her. "Any particular reason why you ought to be wanting to keep Beanbug behind us?"

Pos and Leifford looked down at me, shaking their heads, and Kelsey motioned me to one side with his hand.

The little feist, being ahead of us, just slowed us down, in more ways than one. Near the top of the mountain, Pos got picked across the face by a briar and let out an oath that would have pleased Satan. Beanbug's tail shot between her hind legs, and she squatted and waited for whatever-was-to-come to come. We pulled up and waited. Finally, Kelsey said: "Any idea how long it might take to wear off?"

"She's coming out of it now," Weasel said, humming the making of a hymn which was probably the closest he'd ever been to church.

"But if you don't get that boy to clean his mouth up we'll be all day making it to the ridge!"

Kelsey gave me a look like the oath had belonged to me, and I might not be coming again if I came out with another one. And although he was in front of me, he should have known by the voice that the oath belonged to Pos. But I was biding time until I got a chance to cut down on a squirrel and show them all a thing or two about hunting.

Reaching the ridge, the little feist hadn't gone twenty feet before I knew that she was a bigger hypocrite than the lot of us. I mean, you talk about lying! She barked treed on every tree along the ridge, and we searched for a squirrel in them until our eyes ached. By the time we reached the main grove where the hickories were, none of us pretended to hear her at all, all of us except Weasel. He laid the blame on the noise I was making, scaring the squirrels out ahead of us.

I guess that's why no one except Weasel paid any attention when Beanbug treed on a huge black oak that had had its head knocked off by lightening except for one limb at the top that stretched out like it was pointing down the mountain. It was probably no more than twenty feet from the ground. Time had hollowed out the center of the old tree, taking its heart and leaving only a sliver of sapwood to keep one limb alive.

Beanbug had struck a trail this side of it, followed it to the hollow of the tree, stuck her head in the hole, and yipped with a voice that sounded like it was coming out of a jug. Figuring that Beanbug had lied again, tired from feather-walking for quietness, we pulled up to catch a breather. The little dog was all the way inside the hole by now with only her tail sticking out, swinging like the pendulum on a clock. Weasel dropped to his all-fours and popped the little feist out of the hole with her fighting him all the way to stay in. Once she was out, he squeezed his head inside the hole, twisting his body so he could look up. The Beanbug dog tore at the bark of the tree, tried to climb it, jumping on it and falling off like the hypocrite she was, not fooling me. Finally, Weasel pulled himself out of the hole, letting the Beanbug dog back in.

"Squirrel's there, boys!" he said. "Just like Beanbug has been saying they was all along! Big red squirrel this time not far from the top, holding on to the inside of the tree."

We were all excited!

46

Pos said: "What you figuring, Weasel?"

"Well," Weasel answered, "'pears to me someone has got to shuck up that tree from the inside and poke the squirrel out the top!"

Everyone stared at Weasel. I might have been little enough to have made it, but I knew that Weasel wasn't about to let me do that; I mean there were bragging rights to doing something like that. But his going suited me—especially as anxious as everyone seemed about the squirrel coming out.

"All right," Weasel said. "If it's going to be me, I want you to know this ain't no ordinary hole I have to go up. It'll take time. You ought to be able to hear me scratching and know where I am. Watch and don't let Beanbug follow; there's room for just one as it is. I'll have to pop him out of the hole at the top of the tree. If he's stubborn about coming out, there ain't apt to be a finger's worth of distance betwixt me and that squirrel, so don't shoot at first sight! You might blow my head off! He could even come out riding on the top of my head. If so, I'll ease him out that spur limb which I figure he'll run to the end of and jump to that black gum what's closest. When he reaches the black gum, salt 'im down! Not until! Nothing itchy, you hear! It's got to be the black gum!"

You could hear Weasel scratching around inside the hole something awful. Beanbug was turning her head from side to side, listening but making no sound herself. Just for meanness, I hummed a few chords to a hymn, and she wagged her tail.

When Weasel's scratching told us that he was better than halfway up inside the tree, the cocking of the hammers on the guns drowned it out. I was the only one holding a gun uncocked, afraid that excitement might cause me to make a mistake and fire. I spent my time eyeing the end of the black oak limb and the closest limb of the black gum to it; just where I figured the squirrel would land first. Once there, it would have to be a quick shot before he would be lost from sight, and I wasn't about to go traipsing the ridge following Beanbug while she lied about where the big red had gone.

Well, the red squirrel came out the top of the tree just like Weasel said it might, riding the top of his head pretty as a redbird. Gun barrels swirled into the air like the rising of a covey of quail. The explosions sounded like someone had dynamited the mountain! Three shotguns! All double-barrels, all mule-eared, all twelve-gauge, all barrels going off!

The big red squirrel had to be marked by providence. He scooted out the limb, jumped to the black gum and, blinded mostly by smoke from the other guns, I shot and missed! Both barrels, being excited and all. I watched a small limb from the black gum, hit by my shot, fall to the ground. The red squirrel was out of sight.

And then I heard a mournful scream coming from Weasel and cocked my ears as he slid from sixty to zero down the inside of the tree. The others had laid their guns on the ground and were hurrying to get him out. They pulled; he stretched and then popped out like a rubber band. I saw him quiver, moan pitiful, and then stretch out like rigor mortis had set in. I felt better seeing him quiver again. Pos held his head off the ground, cradling him like a baby and shaking his head, funeral-like. Weasel's beady eyes opened and closed. Beanbug whined and wagged her tail at the sight of Weasel and waited.

And then for no reason that I could think of except for being a boy, Pos pointed his bony finger at me and said: "Egod, you've done shot poor Weasel!"

Beanbug looked at me like she was ciphering-out what had just been said.

"Where you hit, Weasel?" Pos asked, giving me a look that said my job at the store was probably over. Beanbug lost the scripture that said something about turning the other cheek, remembered an eye-for-an-eye, and a tooth-for-a-tooth, caught one of my britches legs with her needle-teeth and ripped it down. I managed to shake the little hypocrite off.

"All over my back!" Weasel said, trying to get to his feet, getting there, but being too humped over to pull his shirt off.

I closed my eyes when Leifford eased the shirt up. I was afraid to look knowing what three mule-eared double-barrels could do, but curiosity got the better of me along with figuring if he caught the full charge, he ought to be blown in two. I took a look, and all I could see were a few scratches that had probably been made on his slide down the inside of the tree. I was happy enough to bust.

48

"Why, you ain't even shot, Weasel!" I shouted.

Well, the next thing I heard was the wailing of the Beanbug dog. When I looked, she was flat on her back, her tail between her legs like it had been stitched to her belly, her eyes closed. I squinted and saw Weasel looking down at the little dog.

"Egod, not only did he shoot me, but he's told a lie big enough to snuff the life right out of poor little Beanbug!"

"Shame!" Pos said. "And the finest squirrel dog I ever saw!"

"A good one all right," Leifford said.

"I'd of made a trade," Pos added. "Cleaned out a shelf if that's what it took!" He squinted down at her, smoke still drifting out of the barrel of his gun. "Just couldn't wait, could you?" looking at me.

"Not only has he blowed me half in two," Weasel said, "But he's rubbed the salt in the wound!" He looked again at Beanbug, as quiet as a real squirrel dog out to be. "She'll likely have to be carried off the mountain!"

"You got more than your share of worry right now, Weasel," Pos said. "We'll take care of the little dog. I'd say the shock has took her squirreling away for good, just like you see sometimes on a gun-shy dog. You couldn't get shed of her for her keep now."

And then, before I saw it coming, Weasel jerked the double-barrel out of my hand, broke it down, flipped the shell casings out and smelled. Some powder smoke was still left inside the barrels.

"Both barrels!" Weasel said.

"Why, you're lucky to be here, Weasel!" Pos answered.

And the next thing I knew, we were on our way off the mountain, Weasel hobbling along on a home-made cane that Leifford had whittled out of a sapling, and Pos giving the Beanbug dog a free ride, her eyes wide open unless she caught you staring at her.

Walking behind, knowing what Weasel could and would do about the shooting on the mountain when he reached town, and knowing what the people in Sourwood could and would tack on to it, by the time we had reached the foot of the mountain, I had decided to become a hermit.

And might have had I not run into Lottie a few days later in Sourwood.

"Got you a dog yet?" she asked.

"No," I answered, sure that she must have heard what had happened over on Nebo by way of Weasel's spreading.

"Well," she said, "Lord hears the prayers of little'ns same as he does big'ns."

She reached down and patted me on top the head, and I squinted off to see if anyone was watching, especially boys.

"You get a chance," she said, "I'd like to have me a mess of squirrel to make some gravy over. Got me a craving for it. Apache and Weasel gone all the time. Wouldn't be any different if they was there, though. Neither one could ever hit the side of a barn and be quiet-like inside a woods. Gone to Blaine this time if the truth's in 'em which it usually ain't. But wherever they went, I made them take back a little pestering Beanbug dog they tried to drop-off on me and did for a short while. Never saw the likes! Spent days pestering my mule, and she'd run from scripture like Satan!"

"I'll come," I said.

She nodded her head and tucked her coat tighter around her bony frame.

50

The Last Picture Show

1

The building that housed the picture show in Sourwood was built of brick and stood near the riverbank where the Sourwood River emptied into the great Ohio. It was close enough to both rivers that you could hear the wind play in the willows and catch the hum of the current as it swirled mournful-like around old snags that stuck above the water polished and whitened by the water and sun. Time, weather, and the rising waters had left the building pale and streaked, with always a brown ring around it showing the last rise of the rivers. Rains had stolen mortar from between the bricks, and the floods had filled the cracks with river muck and planted seeds from the cotton willows there. In spring, the seeds sprouted and hung to the side of the building with roots as tender as bloodroot. The dry winds of summer shook them loose, and they fell like young birds from the nest and lay like small, brown skeletons in open graves along the foundation of the building.

To Caleb and the older boys, the picture show was where the girls were; to young boys and the older people who went there each Saturday, it was the home of Hoot Gibson, Ken Maynard, Buck Jones, Gene Autry, wagon trains, Apache Indians, and others.

The show opened on Saturdays and that was the day everyone in and about Sourwood came to town. The fare was ten cents if you were under twelve and fifteen if you were over. The difference was a bull nickel for a sack of popcorn at Kelsey May's store which was nearby. That was a prize worth trying for, never passing beyond the age of twelve.

While the show opened at noon, the excitement started about an hour earlier. That's when Beulah Whitlock, who owned and operated the show, left her home to open up. Unbeknownst to her, we thought, she was nicknamed Mousey. A mysterious and greedy woman who lived in a small brown-framed house hitched to the foot of Sourwood Mountain. She was frail, thin, and bowed at the shoulders—bowed, we knew, for two reasons: from carrying the heavy sack of coins to the show to make change with and from bending over inside the small cage that jutted out on the front of the show like a forecastle on a paddlewheel. The side and lower half of the cage had been built with wood, and the front, high up, had been penned in with wire with a hole in it for her to reach through and take your money. There was no way she could see what was out there until it was a few feet up. But she had had the front built with wood to keep the river wind off her feet to keep her from catching cold.

We figured her face was pale from sitting in the shade of the cage and from worrying about all the money she had. Her cheeks were bony, her eyes red as pokeberries, and her chin tapered. She did favor a mouse, mostly.

She left her house about an hour before show time carrying her sack and a cane that she used to poke around in the weeds along the path in front of her. Rumor was that she was afraid of snakes but mostly that someone might be hiding-off to snatch her money. She moved slowly, shuffling her feet and then stopping to listen, shuffling her feet and then stopping to listen. Exactly the way a mouse would do. Caleb said that along with fear of snakes and losing her money, her slowness also gave her time to figure out ways to keep us from sneaking in or lying about our age.

No one could remember ever seeing her smile. Her mouth was forever set in a frown. She had never married because she was afraid of ending up with a no-good and losing her money. She was seldom seen in Sourwood except on Saturdays, using the rest of the week to guard her money. But that didn't seem to matter. What she did on weekdays belonged to her; on Saturdays she belonged to Sourwood.

We always knew when she left her house. A boy was always hid-off to run ahead and spread word of her coming. We gathered and waited. Gathered from everywhere—in Sourwood, off the mountain, and out of the hollows. Some were brought in by horse and wagon and dropped off at the show while their mothers shopped about. Kids ranging in age from the crib, to overalls, to gingham. Miss Whitlock had long been the baby-sitter for all of Sourwood and as far away as people could travel and get back home after the show at a reasonable hour.

"Now you mind Miss Whitlock," they would say which always caused Miss Whitlock to cast her eyes at them and frown deeper still. Pestered, she gathered what fare she could and tried to catch the little devils trying to sneak through the door free. They came to her on the bottle, grew climbing the seats inside and crawling on the floor, but stopped under the age of twelve. To Miss Whitlock, that they grew up there was one thing; that they stopped under twelve was another! She set about to catch us; out-foxing her was a bull nickel and a brag. And so while she thought of ways to smoke us out, we thought of ways to chip years off. We hunkered below the wire and raised our hands holding out fare, grateful that she had built the lower half of the cage with wood. Generally, only seeing our hand or the top of our head, all she had to go on was our voice.

She tried to outsmart us by asking particulars. Tried to learn every family in and about Sourwood, number of children and ages of each. But there were too many of us. We had our voices down so pat that brags were as tall as the mountain. Stacy Blanton had gotten in for ten cents at the age of sixteen with a voice just off the nipple. Elwood Puckett got in for under eleven and was cutting wisdom teeth, his older brother Elmer just ahead of him still crying for his ma.

The only trouble for Caleb and the older boys was girls. Caleb fussed. He said that girls under twelve wanted to pass for twenty-one, and that when they got there, they wanted to stop. I thought Caleb was right. They gathered outside the show acting grownupish wearing lipstick, rouge, and lilac perfume. Even under twelve they wanted to go inside at an adult fare. If a boy paid their fare, he could be giving up a bull nickel and a sack of popcorn. If he gave up the popcorn, he lost the girl to someone who had some once they were inside the show. Watching Caleb, I learned one thing for sure: a girl wouldn't sit with a boy inside the show without popcorn. That was the straight of it. They wouldn't try to sneak inside the show, either. They'd put on high heels that caused them to wobble when they walked, paint their face, and go inside older-looking and fancy-like. But that was a problem for Caleb and the older boys when they had no money to pay two adult fares plus popcorn, which was often.

Miss Whitlock was forever trying to come up with new ways to catch us. Like turning the job of watching the front of the show over to Hyford Copley who ran the projector machine from a little room built above the cage and running far enough inside the show to cover the first row of seats from above. Hyford had been well-liked around Sourwood until he took on the extra job. Anytime you saw him along the streets of Sourwood, he would have a crowd around him. For everyone knew that Hyford always scanned the picture reels during the week to patch breaks and such before show time on Saturday, and they tried to coax some of what to expect come Saturday. And he would ladle out some of what was on the screen but stop short enough to make waiting for Saturday harder. We figured Miss Whitlock had put him up to that, but there was always the chance he might slip.

The room where Hyford worked, and that jutted out over top of the cage, had two rounded holes cut in the wall inside the show. He used one hole to shoot the picture through and the other hole to look out to make sure the picture was in focus and lined up on the big screen at the other end of the room. That was job enough—for the big screen that held the picture quivered whenever the door was opened and the wind came in from the rivers. The film seemed to be forever breaking, out of focus, or bouncing off the walls.

Once your eyes adjusted to the darkness, you could often look up and see Hyford's head popping in and out the hole like a woodpecker in a hollow tree. And sometimes, mad because the reel had broken, pot-shots were taken at him with tobacco cuds and river gravels. No one ever figured it could be the fault of the reel; it was always Hyford's fault. He was left between a rock and a hard place. When something was wrong with the picture, he had to use the hole. Sometimes he fought back with what he had the most of: ambeer. Said to be born with a cud in his mouth, he was good at it, and he had an advantage—from high above he could send the ambeer down like rain. Trouble with that was that he rained on the just as well as the unjust. And so everyone went after him. Finally, Miss

Whitlock would leave her cage, strut down the aisle, and threaten to call Fats Peterman who was the constable of Sourwood, and we would all quiet down. Not that we were afraid of Fats—he was pencil-thin and weighed less that a sack of middlings with a name that fit because everyone called a thin man Fats and a tall man Shorty. But we knew that she would send Hyford looking for him, and we would have to wait until he got back for the show to start again.

Hyford's luck changed after he took the second job for Miss Whitlock. She had him cut a hole in the wall of the room above the cage so that he could look down and pick us off at the cage or trying to sneak in the door whenever someone else opened it to go inside. Whenever he'd pick off a lie at the cage or a sneak at the door, he'd stomp his foot on the floor above the cage, and Miss Whitlock would nab us. And it worked—for a while. The first Saturday after he had cut the hole, he picked off eleven. The following he upped that to seventeen. But the third Saturday was our turn. We waited around outside the show until we heard the war hoops inside telling us that the reel was broken or the picture was on the wall, and with Hyford busy elsewhere, we made up for the Saturdays we had lost.

But in the end it was Caleb who bailed us out of the hole in the wall. It happened the Saturday Hyford caught Jody Spurlock, nicknamed Tearbaby because he cried so easily and often that the teacher at Sourwood School made him carry a bottle to catch his tears in. Too big for Miss Whitlock to wrestle outside the show, Hyford had come down to help. You could hear Tearbaby wailing all over town. Now the thing was, Jody had a brother who wouldn't give a hoot for Jody unless he was being picked on by someone older, a lot like Caleb was with me. Jody's brother, Nick, was big and burley and had been shaving since the fifth grade. He could drive a nail in a fence post with a river gravel from as far away as you could see. He came off the mountain where he was cutting wood, stopped by the river for a gravel, and stalked Hyford like a squirrel. When Hyford's head popped out, Nick caught him in the jaw with the gravel, and it left a lump on Hyford as large as a duck egg. Caleb had laid it on Nick about Jody, strong. The hole above the cage was boarded up, leaving Miss Whitlock to think of something else.

Miss Whitlock was smart. She gave up trying to catch us on the outside and came up with a way to make up for what she lost on the outside inside. She had a popcorn machine sent up from Louisville and had Hyford install it inside the show, and then she set a fan behind it and blew the smell of the popcorn out over us. We dug inside our pockets and spent whatever we had, regretting nothing but the empty bottom of the popcorn sack. Easy living was a full sack of popcorn, hard times an empty sack. Whenever her sales dropped off, she just turned the fan up and added the smell of butter to the corn.

Trying to make the corn go further, Caleb and the older boys gave the girls only the white puffs and kept the hardtacks for themselves. And when they got tired of grinding them with their teeth, they fought with them. We made bean shooters out of the hollow limbs of sumac and shot the hardtacks like rifleballs, especially when the reel broke.

But, all in all, Caleb considered the popcorn machine inside the show a favor and a fault. A favor because it would make a girl snuggle—a fault because with the popcorn so close, girls ate more. I couldn't understand why Caleb couldn't see that all the girls were after was the popcorn, especially Molly Perkins, the girl he was struck on. To begin with, she was red-headed and had freckles, both faults. Sitting beside them, I noticed other things about her too: like when there was a shootout on the screen, she'd eat as fast and furious as a Gatling gun, letting the barrel cool only during a love scene. And then she snuggled up to Caleb—then it was my turn to steal from their sack.

Of all the girls for Caleb to turn sweet on, Molly was the worst, I thought especially one night after the show when I heard her quarreling up ahead that I was tagging too close. There was no way she would try to get in the show by acting under twelve. She claimed she was older than she really was and went in society-like. That meant that if Caleb sat with her inside the show, he had to pay two adult fares. Money for popcorn was tacked on to that, sometimes borrowed from me. He walked her home now Saturday nights, and I had to trail behind like I wasn't nowhere at all. And after, he quarreled at me all the way home because I had tagged along and kept him from trying something, never telling me what that something was which was the main reason I was trailing them in the first place, trying to notice little things. And then one night just this side of Molly's house, I heard Caleb whistle like a certain night bird that he told me earlier that would be his way of waving me off because he knew that I would be following him, but that he would not be able to see me. We had used the whistle many times on Mom, and it meant that if we didn't stop what we were doing, we could be in trouble. This night it was to mean that if I didn't stop what I was doing, I could be in trouble. But knowing that it had to be something too exciting to miss if he did whistle, I was willing to take a chance.

I stepped off the path, dodged the light of the moon, and worked my way through the brush until I was close enough to where they had pulled up under a hackberry to see them but hoped they could not see me. I had worried all the way there—not so much that they would see or hear me, but I kept hearing noises in the brush on the other side of the path. Maybe it was varmints; I didn't know.

The big moon was so bright that I could see birds roosting on the high limbs of the hackberry. The night was warm, but as close as Caleb was to Molly, goose-pimples covered me. She stood there tight against Caleb, and he was scouting the brush around him. The moon lit up her red hair, and she rocked from side to side, and then she lifted a hand and touched Caleb on the cheek. She looked at the big tree.

"I like a hackberry, don't you?" I heard her whisper.

"Better than any tree on the mountain," Caleb whispered back, a lie bigger than the mountain itself! Caleb hated a hackberry as bad as I did. They had too many limbs to trim for wood and were harder to split than a rock.

"Want to kiss me?" she whispered.

She closed her eyes and puckered her lips, just like the women were forever doing on the big screen at the picture show. I waited for Caleb to set her straight like Buck Jones or Hoot Gibson. But he didn't. He leaned toward her. But then he stopped. I knew he was casting about the brush outside the circle of the tree. I had the advantage on Caleb: he had to steal looks without Molly knowing it; I was free to look without anyone caring. I did and saw Len Walker and Josh Taylor and several more that I couldn't make out, but knowing the ones that ran around with Caleb, I thought I pretty much knew who they were. They were all trying to sneak up as close as they could, but being so many, they had almost run out of cover. Having the eyes of a squirrel, I knew that Caleb had seen me and the others, too.

"What are you waiting for?" Molly whispered.

I was so excited over whether Caleb would kiss her or not that I was afraid they could both hear my breathing. If he did kiss her, it was certain to be known all over the mountain before the sun set on Sunday with enough ways that it had happened to match the color of the leaves on all the different trees along the mountain in the fall of the year. I watched as Caleb eased backwards instead of forwards to where Molly's lips waited, puckered. Caleb looked off toward the undergrowth around him.

"Too much company around for that!" he said, loud enough to have scared off every squirrel in the woods had we been squirrel hunting.

I could hear Len and Josh and the others scurrying off, tripping and letting out oaths. Molly heard them, too. I watched her hike her skirt up and run off toward her house fast as a rabbit. I held my place, taking a chance that Caleb just might not have seen me. But I should have known that his eyes and ears were too good for that.

"You can come out now," he said.

But I was the only one who did. I could hear rustling in the brush from the other side ,but the noise was going the other way.

Walking down the path behind Caleb, I knew that he was mad. I thought he might be thinking about how the story of it all might come out when the boys who had watched it all got through with it. One thing you could generally count on—it wouldn't be the way it was. I knew what I was thinking: what it might have been like if he had chosen to kiss her!

2

For all the money the popcorn machine made, it was not without fault. While there had always been rats inside the show, the scent of the corn drew them up from the rivers in droves. We had learned to live with the ones that had lived there before the popcorn machine came, figuring they probably had more claim to the old building than we had. They had not been too bad to pester. Old-timers claimed that the rats had come up from the river back when the show building had been a saloon—when the great logs were tied in rafts and poled down the Sourwood River to its mouth where they remained until they were sold and then poled down the great Ohio to either Louisville or Cincinnati. Mountain men had gathered inside the saloon and drunk beer and whiskey and eaten cheese and tidbits along the mahogany bar that ran one full length of the big room. Rats came to nibble the crumbs dropped on the floor. They had become independent enough to try to steal from the top of the bar while men shot at them. They quartered at night under the floor of the building and gnawed holes in the flooring big enough to drop a foot through, smart rats that had learned when the saloon had closed for the night to screw their tails down inside the lamps and steal the lard used for fuel. Old men at Kelsey's laughed and said rats'd screw a tail inside a bottle of whiskey, too, after they had gnawed the cork out and then get drunk as a coon. Got bad to fight.

The banks of the two rivers were tunneled with rat dens. They were always coming up from the rivers. You could see them on the streets of Sourwood. Whenever the rivers rose, you could see them everywhere heading for higher ground. They had holes everywhere around the town in case you got too close.

What the scent of the popcorn didn't do to them, the hardtacks that we shot and fell to the floor did. Their paths, slick as muskrat slides, led from the rivers to the picture show. They tunneled under the foundation and gnawed more holes in the floor, holes that Hyford tried to patch during the week by nailing pieces of tin over them. During the show they ran along the floor, climbed the seats, sprang to the wall, lost footing and fell. You could hear them searching for corn and mischief. We watched and listened, especially girls. For girls had forever been afraid of rats, hiking their skirts and screaming. Caleb said rats made girls sit closer.

The trouble was that with so many rats now, they were everywhere. You had to sit tight and cautious. Let your foot wander far enough to touch a foot next to you, and you got stomped. Lean with the horse Hoot Gibson was riding and let your elbow touch the one next to you, and you might end up catching a haymaker. Let a rat touch a girl, and the squall of an Indian didn't have a chance. Trying to watch the screen and watch out for rats took something away from the picture show.

We fought back two ways, mainly: river gravels and hardtacks, beanshooters and slingshots. We got good enough to score on a rat now and then or at least to chase him toward someone else, girls if we could. And then one Saturday, Al Marcum, who was always there early enough to get a seat on the front row, raised as he watched a big rat strut across the stage below the screen and cut down on him using a gravel in his slingshot as big as a hen egg. If he had scored he could have claimed the reward; he missed and paid the penalty. The big gravel caught Buck Jones and his horse as they rode across the screen knocking off the lower half of Buck's left leg and both of the front legs of the horse. There was not enough screen left for their legs to be tacked back on. And with the posse following too close for Hyford to have time to shut the projector down, they lost legs left and right. Everyone went after Al. Most of them had already seen the show at least twice by now, and they were restless anyway. Al claimed he lost enough meat off one ear to bait a turtle hook.

Some of the rats commoned out enough for us to tack nicknames on, and coaxed on the stage by hardtacks, we nicknamed them there. There was Chief Longtail, a tail so long and held high that it shadowed the screen; Scarface, who had caught a river gravel and showed signs of it; Blindy, who had lost one eye from fighting a hardtack or a gravel. Thinking that I might get one ahead of Caleb, I told him that I was saving money to see if I could have Doc Dinkle fix the rat's eye. Caleb said: "Be wasting your time asking. I done tried that and Doc Dinkle told me he wouldn't work on a rat's eye."

But it was the rat we had named after Miss Whitlock that brought giggles. A prissy little rat that crossed the stage a step at a time. Shuffling a few feet, stopping and listening, shuffling a few feet, stopping and listening.

I named a rat after Molly Perkins but kept that to myself—a plump rat that seemed greedier than the others.

But most of the hardtacks were on the floor of the show, and the rats were thicker there. When the fan was turned up, they went wild.

They squealed and ran along the floor like a wild horse stampede. It excited the rats on the stage, and sometimes they jumped on the screen and climbed until they lost footing and fell. A cowboy hunkered down to wipe sweat from his forehead might end up stroking a rat or might go for his gun and end up with a rat to shoot with.

Young kids inside the show made matters even worse. Left there by their mothers or with an older sister to watch, the older sister sneaking off to sit with some boy once inside the show, they crawled along the floor and kept the rats stirred up. Myrtle Deskin and her brood were the worst of the lot. With enough kids to take up a whole row of seats and another one on the way, they were the worst of all to pester, both rats and us. With two left behind to suck, ten climbed the seats like grapevines. If she had ever weaned one, no one knew about it. Caleb said her boy Tad was old enough to cut firewood and was still on the titty. She always drew a crowd outside the show waiting to get inside. Seeing her titties as big as a cow's sack and a kid hanging from each one, the boys giggled and the girls blushed. Older men with their wives had long ago learned to turn their heads.

The rats finally became so brazen that we had to guard our popcorn sacks. Caught up in the excitement of the show, we learned to keep a hand over our sack of corn. I also learned that I could dribble a hardtack along the floor and pass a rat off on someone else. Also, eating society-like made you harder for a rat to find.

3

While complaints about the number of rats inside the picture show grew, Caleb picked off a rumor that Miss Whitlock was planning to open a new show in Sourwood; that planning to do so had nothing to do with rats, but that word had leaked out on how much money she was making, and that a group in Lexington was planning to open a show of their own in Sourwood. Miss Whitlock figured that two shows here would ward them off. The rumor turned out to be true.

She chose another brick building that faced and was even closer to the two rivers. She brought men in to tidy the building up. Instead of long, wooden benches, she brought in divided seats that folded back whenever someone wanted to get to the seat beyond you. No more sliding across laps and ending up with either a welt on your rear end or a fight. Caleb said some of the girls liked that. Miss Whitlock claimed that the seats were the latest thing, had been designed by a doctor of sorts in Louisville so that people wouldn't have to set bowed over and end up with back trouble.

She brought in a popcorn machine that was guaranteed not to burn corn or leave hardtacks, even though we liked our corn scorched and didn't mind hardtacks. The new show had a larger stage and a bigger screen that wouldn't quiver from river wind. Hyford said that the new projector set its own focus, and you couldn't knock the picture off the screen. No more horses running along the walls or the ceiling—no more Ken Maynard, scooted to a corner, having to shoot with a gun bent like a carpenter's square, the hammer busting the cap on one wall and the smoke coming out the barrel on the other wall.

The screen was large enough to hold all the picture. No more horses running near the ceiling. No more Hyford trying to put the picture back on the screen to keep the horses from being on their sides on the stage or lying in your laps. No more Buck Jones hobbling on bowed legs trying to save a woman cut in half by a crack in the other wall; the woman still alive and smiling!

The new show was no ordinary show. Even the lighting was a brag. Cupped back in the walls, they were fancy and wilted down like a dying candle. Caleb said that pleased the girls. While it didn't guarantee they wouldn't get their rear ends pinched, it gave them time to choose who pinched it. The new show offered Hyford a chance to do something right although no one figured he'd ever get the credit for that.

A scraper was set outside the show to clean shoes on: dirt, mud, and the inside of barns. That would make a difference when the show was heated up by the fancy stove and the heat from the number of bodies she figured would be inside, especially if you came from the barn to the show. And the outside of the show was well lighted. It caught both the glare of the moon off the river and the light from the light bulb hung from above the cage and the door. Miss Whitlock could sit on a cushioned chair inside her cage and see all the way to the bricks below. There would be no way to sneak in or to lie about your age. You had to pay. And that's where her troubles started—adding all the fancies, she claimed, had caused her to have to raise the fare. Fifteen cents for under twelve, including babies, and twenty-five cents for adults. She might as well hung up a smallpox sign. No one went there.

Having so much money invested, she set about to change that. She brought the first showing of all films to the new show, and they played before an empty house. We waited until it was either time to send them back to Louisville or bring them to the old show and make something, and they played before a full house. She tried to mend that by holding the old films over and showing only re-runs, but we went just the same. We didn't have anywhere else to go on Saturdays.

We watched the same films so many times that we came to know the actors well enough to call them by first names. We knew and named every horse on the screen, including wild herds. Myself, whenever the cowboys or Indians crossed a stream, I searched for signs of varmints or good places to make sets with traps. We memorized all the talk and even the whinny of horses, knew where everything was going before it got there, and how life was going to end up for them all.

But, still, Miss Whitlock wouldn't give up; she wasn't apt to on anything with money attached to it. She held a grand opening and gave away free pop and candy. She got the mayor, Shelby Butler, to speak at the large gathering. We drank and ate everything, and Mayor Butler was never elected mayor again. He might as well have put a tax on everyone around Sourwood!

Next, Miss Whitlock turned to wax dummies—something she claimed was popular all over the United States and would be in Sourwood as well. She had them shipped upriver and laid-off in front of the new show. Most were laid-off coffin-like, and they drew a crowd. They looked so real that it was hard to tell if they were dead or just resting in Sourwood for a while. So real that you expected one to move at anytime. She had them changed once a week. Robert E. Lee came for a nice visit and was mourned by all. Abe Lincoln had a harder time of it at first, but being from Kentucky and blood being thicker than water,

63

he wasn't mistreated. Jeb Stuart came and was mourned over, especially by the women who claimed he had been so kind to his dear old mother. Mom said that we were akin to Jeb Stuart, and it hurt seeing your kin laid out like that.

But, all in all, it looked like it might be the cowboys that she brought there that might turn the trick for her. They were generally shipped up to match the film she was showing, and it was sad and mournful to see someone you had known for so long laid out. People started dribbling inside the show to see them alive.

When Miss Whitlock ran out of cowboys and Indians, she brought in dummies almost too scary to look at: Frankenstein, the Werewolf, and the sort. Kids looked and wailed, and no amount of talking could pacify them. They twisted up handles on their mothers' dresses or on the clothing of anyone close enough. The worst of the lot was Myrtle Deskin's brood. They stared the hardest and screamed the loudest. She even got afraid she might mark her next child!

"They hain't made of nothin' exceptin' wax," she told them. "Hair from a mule's tail and nothin' real fer sartin'."

But her boy Sid puckered and said: "They's real, Ma!"

"How come you say that?" she scolded, no cloth left on her dress to screw a handle on.

"Because the flies is a-blowin' em!" Sid screamed.

Sid was right. I mean the flies did come up from the river to pester the dummies, and they lay fly-specked like they had had pepper sprinkled on them.

And then one day someone climbed a willow tree, caught the sun just right and shot Daniel Boone through and through with a sunbeam through a magnifying glass. Melted parts of his body right out of his clothing. Knowing that Miss Whitlock would probably have to pay for that, there was little sympathy for her. There was talk that Miss Whitlock claimed it was an act of nature but that Louisville didn't agree. That they were sending up lawyers to take Miss Whitlock to court, but in the end a settlement was made. Good thing, most felt. Sourwood could say and do what it chose as far as Miss Whitlock was concerned, but Louisville was another matter! The lawyers might have been lucky to have got out of Sourwood with their hides still attached.

With the passing of the wax dummies, Miss Whitlock turned to gospel singers. They came from far and wide to stand on the stage picking and singing, not costing Miss Whitlock a cent, rumor was, because gospel singers made their pay by taking up collections. But that never worked out. We learned that we could sit comfortable-like either under or up a willow and hear their songs the same as inside. They picked and sang to an empty house, mostly. We knew they would come outside sooner or later, and since all gospel groups were funeral-like and friendly, we would get to meet them all.

Finally, Miss Whitlock seemed to repent. She talked of closing the door on the new show forever. We thought she had repented. Caleb said that everything had turned out the way Miss Whitlock had expected it to, that what she wanted to do was show Lexington that a second show in Sourwood wouldn't work, and most everyone would agree with that.

4

By and by, the new show playing before practically an empty house, Miss Whitlock decided to lower the price of admission. It was her personal favor to all her friends around Sourwood and about, and she hinted that she might be willing to make other amends—like not having to clean your shoes and other fancies before you could go in. She talked about less lighting which seemed to please everyone the most. You had more freedom with your hands that way. Caleb said that the older women of Sourwood were against that, but all the young favored it. Boys always chose the dark. Mom said dark matched mischief. Caleb said Mom was from the old days and didn't know the half of it.

But even with these changes, only a handful of people showed. Rumor was that the town was about divided equally on reason: half that she hadn't repented enough, the other half that she needed more so she wouldn't do it again.

And yet through it all, Miss Whitlock was not one to give up easy. She tried one more thing: a raffle. She had tickets printed up with the same number printed on either end and when you bought one, she tore the ticket in half, gave one half to you and tossed the other end into a wide-mouthed clear jar so that the tickets she had sold could be seen by all, and you could be sure your ticket stub was in there. She kept the jar set up on the stage too far away for anyone to read off the numbers from the tickets inside but close enough to tease.

The jar sat there under the stares of a goodly crowd until show closing time which was well after darkness had come to the mountain. With all lights turned on inside the show, Miss Whitlock called up someone from the audience to reach in and draw out the ticket that held the winning number. The holder of the matched stub won five dollars. Five dollars! Most saw no end to what that much free money would do; rumors to what it *did do* went beyond that! For one thing, keeping the lights on, showing up who the winner was, and then keeping them on until the winner walked up the aisle and made it outside the show for a running start proved both a favor and a fault. I mean, keeping the lights on until the draw was made and the winner came up on the stage to collect was a had-to-be, but the walk up the aisle exposing him to the near-sighted, far-sighted, and half-blind was another! It gave everyone a shot at him, or her. For five dollars most people around Sourwood would have stolen from their mother!

But Miss Whitlock claimed that to douse the lights earlier might cause someone to trip or fall and get hurt, and she didn't want that worry on her mind. Even though she never turned lights on when the show was over at the old show. Rumor was that with the lights out, she feared a free-for-all! Caleb said that this was one time rumor hit the nail right on the head. And so with the lights you were rich for at least the distance from the stage to the outside door. Once in darkness, you were fair game. Scary and exciting. Something most people liked to take chances on, or, better still, liked to see other people take chances on. Caleb said that your chances of making it all the way home with the money ran from thin to thinner. But if you did make it, you were next to rich and a hero to all the girls, being that money was what girls took to, mostly.

You could reach up and pick off a rumor like a soot tag around a coal stove. Money did strange things, causing suspicion. Some claimed Miss Whitlock already knew who the winner would be before the ticket was drawn from the jar; that she had made a deal to get part of it back and that whoever won, not every time so that you could get a fix on it, but now and then, would slip off to a hiding place inside the front of the show so that they wouldn't stand a chance of being mauled and robbed outside and gave Miss Whitlock back her share, and yet no one could tell you to save them where the hiding place might be.

With thoughts that it was rigged, kin turned against kin and even brother against brother—like during the Civil War, maybe worse, being this was Sourwood. Everyone was under suspicion. Which played right into Miss Whitlock's hands. Pure and simple: the new show was now playing to an overflow crowd, not necessarily for what was on the screen, but the excitement of seeing who the *unlucky* winner would be. Mom fussed at Caleb more than once, whenever she was within hearing distance, of a rumor he was passing on to me about what had happened to the last winner down at the show. Most of them, Mom claimed, made Frankenstein a Sunday school teacher, but Caleb said that Mom was only trying to spare me since I was younger than him. Mom said that Caleb's imagination was wilder than a mountain wind.

Believing Caleb was more exciting, and sticking with him was the best way to go. I mean, being able to go, money-wise. Caleb had got him a job working for Elias Skaggs up Sourwood Creek, a few miles from home, and he was willing to pay my show fare which I was to pay back if and when I won and if and when I made it home with it or else later on from wild game I sold. If I couldn't make it home, or didn't pay in the end, then he got my mule-eared shotgun. That wasn't hard to agree to, especially about winning the raffle and getting mauled. I had heard Mom say that your chance of odds-on winning was like finding enough blackberries on a bush to bake a pie in December. Miss Whitlock never gave anything away and never to the church while there was still time, instead squirreling it all away where Satan would find it in the end—or, some lucky boy coming up with where she had hid it off, mainly like him, Caleb said.

To spread a little more honey close to the hive, Miss Whitlock started giving the winnings out in one dollar bills instead of a single five. This stretched it out to be like more than it really was—counting slowly to allow greed to set in. It was an old trick; I mean five ones would beat a single five anytime. That's why Kelsey May sold by the quarter pound instead of a miserly four ounces.

But rumors marched on fast and furious, with Caleb bringing almost more than he could carry by way of the men he saw at Elias Skaggs's. It made it all frightening and exciting. I mean not only the winner might be in deep trouble once he stepped out into the darkness of the mountain, but his kin as well. For the rumor had spread that some of the winners had been passing their winnings off to a member of the family or even a trusted friend to sneak home for them. And so now, mostly, Caleb said he had heard at Elias's no one was claiming kin to anyone.

Well, that's where Caleb and I drew the line! I mean, we lay awake nights talking about it. I mean what times Caleb wasn't talking about gamecocks, especially the one he planned to own one day to make him rich by.

"I thought it was girls you mostly wanted," I said, trying to turn him back to how we would hang together if ever one of us won, instead of talk on chickens.

"Same end," Caleb answered, "just a different path to take. It all ends up being rich, and that brings on all the girls you want."

I figured it was the same with hound dogs, and so I couldn't argue with that.

But eventually we always got back to talking blood kin. We took an oath that whichever one of us won, we would never deny the other: I mean, deny your own brother!

Well, the way it was turning out, it looked like a winner ending up a loser was striking it rich for Miss Whitlock. People came not so much to win as to see who might and have to fight his way home. Whether it was plain robbery by some drifter up from the river or your next-of-kin who lifted the five, it had now turned into a game, the best game in Sourwood, Caleb said. Sourwood was like that, Caleb said; whatever it was, if they couldn't have it, they didn't want anyone else to.

And so there everyone sat Saturday night watching while some poor soul's number was called, watching him give away signs of a win by squirming in his seat the closer the numbers on his ticket matched. And then either standing up on his own because of the power of money or being given away by someone behind him who had leaned over the back of the seat when the signs showed and had given the winner's name away by yelling it out loud enough to make it out the door of the show and probably all the way across the big Ohio River. Either way, all eyes watched as the poor winner slowly made his way to the stage, being pulled by the devil in the form of an invisible rope made of five one-dollar bills. It did no good to look pitiful, down-and-out, or even crippled-up. A crowd like this was apt to maul a member of their own family! Caleb said Elias told him that if the violence didn't cut down, Miss Whitlock stood to lose it all.

Well, for some reason bad luck is always something you figure to happen to someone other than yourself. Someone, say, like poor Caleb. I mean, the night he won the raffle instead of me. How quickly your past can come back to haunt you. Like, how if it was to ever happen to either of us, we would tough it out through thick and thin. We had planned ways to beat the others and make it home with the money that sounded good at the time but that I figured didn't stand a chance at this moment. Here we were, sitting side-by-side, blood brothers until that last number was called, and then I didn't even know who the boy sitting beside me was, but whoever, there would be no passing off greenbacks to me!

Making it even more pitiful, Caleb and I had been getting along so well. He'd had a falling-out with Molly, and her name was never even being brought up when we went to the show. He shared his popcorn with me. He had even talked about how when he won all the money, and had got that big champion gamecock, he might even send off and order me one of those long-eared hound pups you saw in magazines where they ran after mountain lions and the sort. He laughed about what little chance a coon would have against a dog like that! I'd be the "cock of the walk" and could show them all then, especially Weasel!

Actually, a forewarning that the night was to belong to Caleb came early. I felt him squirm after the first three numbers were called and scooted a little farther away. And Elzy Ward, who was so old that he had lost all his teeth but for some reason still had the eyes of a squirrel, sat just behind us. He had also picked up Caleb's squirming at the call of the fourth number, and his humping over his seat had pinned a few more eyes on Caleb.

69

It happened so fast! When the fifth number was called Elzy was on his feet pointing toward Caleb and calling his name which, I thought, turned poor Caleb some favor since, without teeth, most of what Elzy said most times was hard to make out, got garbled somewhat.

Scooting as far off as I could without going out of my seat and into someone else's lap, and trying to dodge the pitiful stare Caleb was trying to pass off on me like I had been the one he had chosen to carry his last words home to Mom, I felt a finger from behind tap me on the shoulder. I looked around and didn't recognize the old man who was doing the tapping. Come to think of it, I probably wouldn't have recognized my own mom right then.

"What did they say the boy's name was?" he asked, just as Caleb was making his way to the aisle to take hold of the greenback rope Satan used to pull greed to the stage.

I squinted at Caleb now that there was some distance between us. He looked ghost-white under the big spotlight that covered him like an invisible cone and shuffled him forward. He looked much older than I remembered him being, and I had never seen him walk so cripple-like. It was like he had grown old right before my eyes. I looked at the old man who continued to tap me on the shoulder.

"Beats me!" I answered.

"I wonder who the poor boy is," he said. "He was sitting by you."

"Never saw him before in my life," I answered, loud enough—for shame—so that others could hear me.

I stepped out of the show just as the lights went out. I loafed-off in the shadows under the willows near the edge of the big river, found too many people there for some strange reason, and worked my way to higher land to wait around before turning toward home to allow time for whatever was to happen to poor Caleb to happen. I had denied my own brother!

But just this side of home, what I had done became too unbearable. Figuring that I could not desert poor Caleb and carry his haint on my back the rest of my life, I turned back down the path.

I hadn't gone more than a hundred yards before Caleb dropped off of a tree limb that hung over the path and joined me.

"You look white as a ghost!" he said, laughing.

It took me a moment to catch my breath. I was happy and curious enough to bust.

"How did you do it?" I said, telling what I said loud enough for all the mountain to hear.

"Simple," Caleb said. "Went to the old river plan that I had talked about. Waited until enough people had poured out of the show and then threw the log into the river like I was going to swim my way to being rich in Ohio," Caleb laughed. "Ought to be a number of 'em reached the Ohio shore by now."

And then remembering that Caleb had let me pass by him on my way home, I said: "How come you let me walk under the tree and pass you?"

"Just wanted to see if we was still brothers through thick and thin," Caleb said. "When you turned and came back, I knew you had gone looking, and we was brothers for sure!"

This side of the house Caleb reached inside his pocket and pulled out the greenbacks. He peeled two off and handed them to me.

"Just like we took oath," he said, "we split right down the middle."

Knowing that the middle was fifty cents away, I stuck the greenbacks inside my pocket as payment on a hound dog and said no more; I was too happy to know that Caleb had beat the odds. Even more happy that I had turned back to pick up the pieces. And, come to think of it, I seemed to remember that I was the one who thought of throwing the log in the river; had even put the log there and showed Caleb where it was. But, let it be.

Mom said she never heard of anyone getting waylaid over the money in the first place—that it had been nothing but rumors. But I chose to believe Caleb; it was more exciting that way.

Between Girls and Gamecocks

1

After the closing of the new show, Caleb got me a job with him working for Elias Skaggs, actually two jobs: working in corn weekdays and on weekends working up at Elias's barn where gamecock fights were held.

"Make sure you stay in the bottomland instead of up the hollow," Mom said. "Remember too, that no one has made a penny yet off of Elias that he ain't got back. Money never leaves him, for sure."

It sounded something like Apache all over again, but I was too excited about my new job to dwell on it.

Working in the fields of corn in the bottomland along Sourwood Creek gave me a chance to check the creek for muskrats and mink for winter trapping. With the fields of corn running along the creek, and high mud banks most of the way, the muskrats had gathered there. They dug their entrance to their holes under water and then turned them up inside the bank where their nest would be dry. Corn blades and grass stuck out of many of the holes and, caught by the current, quivered like snakes. Muskrat slides down the bank were everywhere, and knowing that several muskrats generally used the same slide to get from bank to water, I knew there were lots of muskrats there. And wherever there were muskrats, mink traveled also. I searched the banks during breaks for places to set traps later on when cold weather came to prime their hides.

I figured to use some of the money from trapping to buy more traps and run even a longer line so that I would make more money to buy me a hound dog pup that would grow getting attached to me and not someone else.

"Know what?" Caleb asked me one evening while we worked our way up a long row of corn. Before I could ask what, he added: "Elias says if I work hard and long enough he might let me have a gamecock of my own at a fair price. One with the bloodlines of a real champion!"

Well, from that day forward it was gamecocks up one row of corn and gamecocks down another; gamecocks when we stopped to eat or rest, all the way home, and even when we went to bed at night.

Talk of game chickens around Sourwood was nothing new. The only thing that made it different now was that it was coming so fast and furious from Caleb. Talk of them was everywhere in Sourwood. Many were kept in pens or out-buildings in the town proper. Even the mayor was known to keep a few in a jail cell overnight at times or during flood-time from the two rivers, with the chief of police having a few of his own in a cell far enough away so that they could not spar one another or the mayor's between bars.

Not all game chickens were in pens. Many were hatched, raised wild and lived on the mountain thick as grouse. But mixed on the mountain, there was no way to know for sure what the mix might be, if it would be game mix or, heaven forbid, that the mix might include the blood of culls such as Leghorns, Rhode Island Reds, Domineckers and the sorts, all cowards when it came to fighting, especially at the touch of a steel gaff.

But there were stories of how once-upon-a-time, a great champion had been plucked off the mountain by someone who had believed that all gamecocks deserved at least a chance just like Kelsey did when it came to dogs. But the chance of finding a winner along the mountain wasn't great enough to put money on or cause men to go searching. The only thing you could be sure of if it was pure game was that it would fight, either winning or dying, but never quitting. And not only was this true among gamecocks but among hens as well, especially if she had a brood at her side. Laying, hatching and raising broods were all the hens were ever used for. Even Mom, who believed that to fight chickens was a mortal sin, believed that game hens were the finest mothers of all the chickens on the mountain. And more than one person around Sourwood kept game hens—but not roosters—for just that purpose, brood hens to nurture their cull biddies for protection around

74

dogs, cats, weasels, fox, mink and other chicken-eating varmints that got brazen enough to come into town.

I had learned of the bravery and courage of the game hen myself just the summer before.

I was on the mountain gathering huckleberries when I stepped out of a grove of trees and saw the hen fighting the red fox. Squinting into an evening sun, I saw that she was no larger than a bantam and that her feathers were black as midnight. I knew that she was a Warhorse, a game breed of chicken common on the mountain and often as wild and untamed as grouse. I knew, also, that she, like I said, was not a chicken Mom had tacked many favors on. Mom judged game chickens bred for fighting too small and tough for frying and no fat for dumplings. The hens had a habit of sneaking off along the mountain to hatch and raise their brood, seldom bringing them to coop. By day, she scratched them a living along the rugged slopes and, shortly after feathering, coaxed them to the limbs of trees where they roosted at night like wild birds. I had, however, heard Mom say that talk was the Warhorse made the finest of brood hens, fierce mothers with a courage to defend their young against all odds. Caught with her unfeathered brood in an open patch of land by the red fox, she had chosen to make her stand.

I watched as the small hen dropped a wing and scooted backwards across the rugged land, coaxing the fox to follow. I knew that she was pretending hurt and an easy catch. More than once I had watched wild birds do this to coax danger from their young. But her movement was slow and awkward. Shielding my eyes from the sun with the palm of my hand, I saw that she had lost a leg. I watched the red blood drip from her black feathers. She had been fighting the red fox for some time now, and she was losing. She was no match for the red fox, and I could not understand why she had not flown to the limbs of a tree for her safety. She could have lived to raise another brood.

Her scheme to lure the fox by dragging her wing did not work this day. The fox, perhaps sensing that she was his on a want, seemed more interested in finding where she had hidden her brood. He lifted his nose into the air and scented toward a tuft of grass nearby. Almost in a crouch, he tiptoed toward it.

The hen, frantic now and squawking pitifully, dragged toward him. Reaching the fox, she pecked at his haunches, and when he turned, she shuffled and filled his face with feathers. He grabbed the hen with his sharp teeth and flung her into the air. She landed a few feet away. Flopping to gain balance, she dragged toward him again. But the fox, paying her no attention now, hunched his back, sprang, and landed near the tuft of grass. He chewed and swallowed, and I thought that he had caught one of the biddies. He hunched and sprang again and again.

Pushing herself sideways with one leg, the hen reached the fox again. She filled his face again with feathers and then, pushing herself away and squawking, coaxed the fox to follow. The fox stared toward her, and I saw blood dripping from the end of his nose. Slowly he moved toward her.

Sensing that the temper of the fox had worn too thin, I grabbed a rock and ran toward them, yelling to the top of my voice. I heaved the rock. Startled, the fox stared toward me, but hearing the fall of the rock close by, he grabbed the hen, threw her over his back, and ran toward a gully, but not before I had been able to see that she was still alive. As the fox ran, I saw the entrails of the little hen bouncing along the fox's back.

Knowing that she still lived caused me to run faster. Briars and brush slashed my face, and blood and sweat itched and blinded me. I blinked to clear both from my eyes.

Near the gully the fox was slowed by a patch of wild honeysuckle. I searched for another rock, determined that if the hen died, the fox would not eat her. Finding a rock, I threw it and caught the fox on his haunches. The fox dropped the small hen and disappeared into the gully.

I wiped my eyes with my arm and tried to clear them. I walked slowly to where the hen lay. She blinked her eyes and quarreled softly. I picked her up, cradling her in my arms. A bone stuck through a broken wing, one leg had been slashed off, and she jerked as I pushed her entrails back inside her. She tried to peck but was too weak. Blood dripped out of her bill. With tears blinding my sight, I wanted to tell her that I would not hurt her, that she was safe from the fox, but I knew that I could not do that.

I carried her back to where she had hidden her brood, and, cup-

76

ping out a shallow hole with the heel of my boot, I placed her in it—a bed where she could die.

Watching the eyes of the little hen opening and closing slowly, I thought of her brood. I wanted to tell her that if any were left, she had no fear, that I would leave them to the mountain as she had intended, but I knew that she would not understand that either. To the small hen, I knew that I was the same as the red fox.

She lay there, unable to live and unable to die. Time-caught. I was determined that I would stand a deathwatch by her so that she would not die alone. And as I watched the slow opening and closing of her eyes, I wondered again why it was that she had chosen to challenge the fox knowing that she could not win—to save a few scraggly biddies, most of which would be lost to the mountain anyway.

At sunset, I walked to where she lay and touched her with my fingers. The only movement was the slow blinking of her eyes. The night wind came to the mountain and jelled the blood on her feathers.

When the trees along the mountain were no more than outlines before my eyes, the small hen died. I broke a stob from a tree and started gouging out a grave for her. I heard a rustle behind me and turned to watch a single black biddy scurry from the tuft of grass and burrow under the dead hen for warmth and protection. I swallowed. If I can catch it, I thought, I might keep it, and then I thought of the promise I had made to the hen—a promise that I would not touch her brood. I thought, too, of what might happen if Mom could tell it was game, but as I dug, the want to keep grew strong.

When I lifted the hen to carry her to her grave, I did not have to make that decision. The biddy disappeared in a blur, and in darkness I knew that I would never find it. Darkness had stolen away my knowing which would have won—the want or the promise.

I buried the little hen on the mountain and placed a flat rock over her grave to keep varmints from digging her up. I broke the stob and made a crude cross, pushing it into the hard earth. Getting my bucket of huckleberries, I came again to the grave of the black hen and stood staring. Wondering why it was that so many things I had tried to help along the mountain had had to die. Small birds that had fallen from their nests, young rabbits caught in storms, and once, a small hairless possum that had fallen from the pouch of its mother and that I had tried to keep alive by feeding it milk through a straw. I remembered how Mom had said that even my helping often left human scent and caused whatever it was to be an outcast among its own kind, and maybe caused death. I remembered her saying that it had been written that for all things living, there was a time for dying, and while I did not understand, this was the only answer she had.

I turned slowly down the mountain hoping that the redness would leave my eyes and not shame me in front of Mom or Caleb.

In the fall, which was when the heavy fighting took place at Elias's barn, you could pick up fresh talk of gamecocks almost anywhere around Sourwood, especially at Kelsey May's general store. Old-timers whittling there turned most of their talk to game roosters. They told how, once toughened for the pit, a gamecock was just this side of blue steel. And now and then, if a boy was around, an old man would show his broken teeth and swear the teeth got that way from trying to eat a gamecock. Swallow a piece and not even Doc Dinkle could help you, generally. The leg of a gamecock, pit-ready, could be used as a hammer, a blackjack, or the handle for a door. The hide of a gamecock made better bootlaces than the hide of a groundhog. Nightshade Coulter, coffin-maker and undertaker in Sourwood, was said to use bits and pieces to plug holes in coffins to keep water out. The plugs could be sanded, planed, lacquered, or left natural. Lon Chaffins, who whittled at Kelsey's, claimed that Doc Dinkle had treated him for gall stones for almost two years before he learned that Lon had eaten most of a seven-time winner that had been killed inside the pit. Lon claimed the gizzard was still laying-off there, refusing to be whipped by anything Doc Dinkle could throw at it.

Old men spoke of three breeds: the Dom, Roundhead, and Warhorse. The right cross of the three was better than the pure of either. Catch it just right, and you had a champion. There was only one exception that they knew of: a big black Warhorse that belonged to Elias Skaggs and was named Blackjack. Outsiders could testify to that.

The Dom was the larger of the three. Mottled as gray as a melting snow, he was a slugger, a toe-to-toe rooster that tried to bully his way on size and strength alone. But what he gained on strength, he lost on slowness. The Roundhead was the shuffler of the mountain. A small, pretty rooster quick as a cat and as red as a dying sun. From a stand he could rise like a ball of fire, hang like a hummingbird, and drop down on the back of another rooster. But what he gained on quickness, he lost on size and power. The Warhorse was as black as midnight. He was the gutsiest of all the gamecocks, knowing no fear of rooster, varmint, or even man. Inside the pit he had been known to fight both man and rooster. But what he gained on bravery, he often lost to carelessness.

One night, tired from working in corn all day, Caleb turned in bed, raised on an elbow and whispered: "Funny. I used to think girls were the prettiest thing in the world. But they ain't!"

"What is?" I whispered back.

"A gamecock!" Caleb said.

I never answered. I was too sleepy. Besides, I knew that Caleb had been wrong on both: the prettiest thing had to be either a hound dog or a trapline.

And I might have always believed that, if Caleb's talk of gamecocks hadn't got around to talk of money—how the right rooster might make enough money to buy enough traps to run a trapline to Kingdom Come and back and a hound dog to boot. Using hindsight, maybe Caleb saying that was to get me to listen with more excitement to his gamecock talk, the rooster *he* would one day own. Whatever, what he didn't know was from that day forward, I started plotting for a rooster of my own.

As we shocked corn, Caleb was more anxious than ever to talk of gamecocks, and I was more anxious to listen, but trying not to show it. My listening pleased him. Me too; I knew that if I was going to own a champion, I needed to know all I could about them in general. I was greedy, greedy for the best. Like Blackjack, the big Warhorse owned by Elias Skaggs!

Me being a good listener, Caleb laid it on me. He was greedy to talk. He had to hide his talk from Mom, keep it from the boys he loafed with, afraid they might try to get ahead of him, and that rounded it out to me. To be sure that I would keep his secret, he sweetened the pot, told me that he'd probably end up letting me have some of his earnings to buy more traps.

He told me one evening that you had to allow a young rooster to run loose for a while until he became a stag—about half grown. That built his wind and strengthened his legs.

"But wouldn't you be afraid a fox might catch him?" I asked.

"You don't let him go high on the mountain," Caleb answered. "You got to watch him. But, if he did, that's a chance you take; the mountain separates the strong from the weak."

Just beyond the age of a stag, the rooster's comb and waddles were trimmed so that another rooster could not grab and hold on to them inside the pit. Both were bad to bleed and blind a rooster. You could trim them with a sharp razor or, better yet, bite them off with your teeth like an old woman trimming the fingernails of a baby. While he healed, you trained him for the pit—things like pulling him forwards and backwards, flipping him from side to side, and then throwing him high in the air to teach him to land on his feet each time. You trimmed his spurs and fitted him with a gaff, watching him fight a cull rooster to determine what sort of gaff he would need. If he fought low to the ground and struck coming up, he was fitted with a "jagger gaff," the shorter of the two and curving more toward the end. If he struck coming down, he was fitted with the "needle gaff," long, slender, and with no curve. Both gaffs had one thing in common: they were honed to a razor's edge.

Before his fight, his food and water were rationed out. Especially water. Too much and he was a "wet" chicken; too little and he was a "dry" chicken. Either way he was a dead chicken!

Knowing how Mom felt about game chickens, I wondered how we would be able to get our roosters home. But knowing that Caleb would probably get his rooster first, I figured to watch and find out.

2

Starting to work at Elias's barn, we came home early mornings puffed out with game talk. We had been able to stay out late by telling Mom that Frank Hatcher had traded for a coondog and that he wanted us to help with the training. Mom never objected to our being on the mountain; she judged that better than our being off in Sourwood. She told us it would be all right, but that she hoped we wouldn't shoot the coons out of the trees since she had heard they were getting scarce.

During the day we set about talking about the goings-on at Elias's barn. The pit where the roosters fought had been built inside the barn with oak boards that had been soaked in the creek until they would bend without breaking. Then the boards were bowed in a circle and nailed so that they would hold that shape. The fighting pit was two feet tall and perfectly round. The floor had been covered with sawdust and stomped solid. We had helped do that. The old sawdust was stained red from the blood of roosters, and Elias wanted to clean it out. A single light bulb hung from a joist over the pit but high enough to be missed by a high-flying rooster. A set of scales hung from a post where roosters could be weighed and matched to the ounce unless a fighter wished to give or take weight.

Having heard some strange tales about handlers down at Kelsey's, I asked about them.

Caleb frowned at my ignorance and shook his head.

"You got to have a handler," he said, "unless you want to handle yourself, which few people do. With the size of a bet running as high as a dirt farm or as low as a man's woman, a good handler can make the difference. Handling is all some men do up there, like Weasel and Blinddog Alley."

Each rooster had to have a handler. The handlers took the roosters inside the pit, held them close enough to peck at one another and madden-up, and then turned them loose. Handlers also stood close by to separate the roosters if they hung gaffs, or, if fought by rounds, try to bring an injured rooster back. Things like if the rooster was bleeding out of the bill, you blew up his rear-end.

"That's called 'cleaning the pipes,'" Caleb grinned. "Ain't bad if you don't suck in."

With every fight one thing was for sure: one rooster would die. Either by the other rooster or by the handler for not making a good fight of it. If a rooster should choose to run, which a pure game seldom did, he was fair game to anyone who could catch him, generally by someone sitting in the spiraled seats around the pit; seats that reached almost half-way to the top of the barn. Caught, his neck was wrung. No one wanted to chance a brood from a coward.

Caleb said that if he chose a handler, he'd probably go with Blinddog Alley. Weasel was good, weasel-quick, but Blinddog was said to be able to talk to roosters. He was one-eyed; he had lost an eye one night to a big Dom that he was handling inside the pit. The big Dom had won his fight, and Blinddog, having had too much to drink, dropped to his all fours and shuffled in the sawdust like he was aiming to take the big Dom on himself. That suited the Dom fine. With one shuffle, he caught Blinddog's eye with a steel gaff and cored it out like coring an apple.

I went to sleep that night sure of one thing: I'd get me a handler.

3

The fights were held Friday and Saturday nights, and I was excited about my job there, especially after Caleb and I had come home the first week with a sawbuck that we had earned, and especially when he told me the sawbuck was only the beginning. He lived only in a world of happiness, bragging about all the money he would have once he had his own champion. He spoke carelessly about his money, giving some here and some there, and even dropping off a little to the Slaboak Church for payment of getting to go there Sunday nights to flirt with the girls, me trailing along to watch. But his offering to give money to the church scared me. I had soaked up enough scripture to know that was mockery, and I knew the penalty for that.

Our job at the barn was dry-picking roosters that were killed inside the pit. Too tough to eat and no fat for dumplings, owners seldom if ever claimed them, and so Elias took them all. He sold them off to Beans Dawson who owned a fancy restaurant in Sourwood and Beans ground them up into chicken salad and sold them off to the uppities without their knowing. His chicken salad was a brag around Sourwood.

Caleb said the job would probably end up meaning a rooster for him, that he had bargained with Elias to hold his pay back as down-payment on one. With no money of his own from working, Caleb spent most of his time on our way home from the barn trying to borrow money from me—told me he'd double the loan once he got his rooster. But what Caleb didn't know was that I was saving money for a rooster of my own, and that worried me. I would need money for trapping, also. Greedy, I had started thinking about trying to catch me a rooster off the mountain and saving my money. I tried to smoke Caleb out on that.

"Why don't you just catch you a rooster off the mountain?" I asked.

"Forget it!" Caleb said, disgusted-like. "Them roosters are as hard to sneak up on as crows. Besides, the good ones are probably being watched. You could end up with one mixed with cull and that means a coward every time. All he'd know to do would be run from a fight. And there you'd be: a hole knocked in the bottom of your poke and your own rooster to pick. That's sad!"

But it wouldn't be sad for me. After working at the pits, I had decided not to fight my rooster. I mean, I had lain awake nights thinking about dry-picking a rooster that I had become attached to. The way I had it figured, all I had to do once I had my rooster was to close my eyes and pull up the necessaries. If I wanted a champion, I'd have a champion. That had always worked for me before. As simple as being an Indian chief or a cowboy. Oh, I might bring him down off the mountain where I'd have him penned and let him whip up on Mom's big Dominecker a time or two while she was gone into Sourwood. I didn't like her Dominecker anyway. She did, and she had named him Prettytom, but he was bad to catch you gathering eggs and not looking, and shuffle on your behind.

Still pestering Caleb about a rooster on the mountain, I said: "Maybe you could scoot out a limb where he's sleeping at night and grab one."

"Just shows how little you know about gamecocks," Caleb frowned. "Pure gamecocks sleep with one eye open. He'd fill your face with feathers and knock you off the limb before he flew away like a night hawk."

"Be better to get him during the daytime," I said. "You could see what you got that way."

Caleb frowned and set his eyes on me.

"And just how do you do that Mr.-game-rooster-man?" Caleb asked.

I was remembering a story Hyford Bailey, one of the old-timers down at Kelsey's, had told one day about a man he knew named Sam Adkins whose wife always sent him on the mountain to catch a fat rooster whenever company was coming. Sam had a sure-fire way. He just sized up the rooster he wanted and started it walking up ahead of him—kept it going, through brush, up and down the slopes, and across gullies. Walked it into the next county if he had to. He never let it stop to rest. Next thing you knew, the rooster would become so tired and disgusted with walking that he'd be glad to be carried back and end up on the table.

"Well," I said, "I'd just catch me a rooster like Sam Adkins does."

"Ain't no truth to that one," Caleb said, letting me know he had heard the story, too.

"How come?" I asked.

"Get a rooster mad before he ends up on the table, and he ain't worth eating," Caleb said. "Same with a hog. Makes their meat too strong."

And I thought that Caleb could be right. I had heard old men say that a hog riled before killing wasn't worth scrapping.

Most of Caleb's talk was on the rooster he was earning. His brag was as big as the mountain—like owning a rooster more than enough for old Blackjack! A rooster he wouldn't choose to fight though because Elias had been so good to him. Besides, old Blackjack meant too much to Elias for Caleb to allow his rooster to kill him. I knew that it took nerve for Caleb to be thinking things like that. I mean everyone knew that Blackjack was the best on the mountain. No one local would even dream of matching against him. It took an outsider to do that, one that had never heard of him and sometimes a greenhorn at that. Many a greenhorn had been weaned off on old Blackjack. From any way you looked, Blackjack was a cleaner-upper. Knowing he could not match him local, Elias would wait until strangers came, and he'd match their roosters with a fair-to-middling one and lose. Just when it looked like he'd lost everything, he'd stagger in with Blackjack for one more fight, a winner-take-all. And take all Elias did.

Elias scared me anyway. His temper was as sharp as a gaff. His voice was rough and final, always on the number of roosters he said we had picked on a given night, a count that Caleb always complained about on our way home over the mountain.

One Saturday evening when we had gone to the barn early to clean up, Elias called Caleb to one side and said: "I might have a rooster for you by the end of next week." He looked closely at Caleb. "You sure you ain't got a little money hid back?"

"No," Caleb said, and I could tell he was almost too excited to talk. Elias scratched his beard.

"Appears to me like you got a man's want and a boy's poke," he said. And just when it looked like poor Caleb would drop, he added: "Could be you'd have to work some longer without drawing pay. Depends on what sort of rooster you want." He studied Caleb. "What sort?"

"Something like akin to Blackjack!" Caleb said, just like that! Elias only grinned.

"Got rooster sense, ain't you?" Elias chuckled. "Could be you'd work the winter for something like that."

"I'd be willing," Caleb said.

"I'll go looking," Elias said. "Don't generally let Blackjack stock go." He scratched his beard again. "But, I was a boy once. Growed up hard. Ain't no reason it ought to be that way with you. I mean, getting weaned off too early."

We crossed the mountain that night with Caleb counting his money and me thinking he could work his life away at the pit.

4

The following Saturday night after we had picked our last chicken, and the crowd had left, Elias stepped inside the back door of the barn and motioned for Caleb. I followed from a distance and watched them step off into the darkness. I could hear them walking and knew that they were headed for the long row of cages where Elias kept his roosters penned. I stepped into the darkness and walked closer, but not too close. Elias had been drinking heavy, and I was afraid of him. I listened and knew that they had reached the pens. The mountain was quiet except for the quarreling of the roosters. Finally, I heard Caleb yell: "Ouch!" I heard the ruffle of feathers, and then Elias laughed. Hearing them coming back toward the barn, I backtracked and waited. I saw them caught in the thin beam of light that seeped through a crack in the barn door. Caleb was holding a rooster.

"Hold that rooster tight," Elias said. "Don't you be letting him get loose on you along the mountain. He'll go looking for something to fight night or day; enough Blackjack in him to do that!"

"He's something!" I heard Caleb say.

"And mean," Elias added. "Don't know why I'm parting with some of my best stock except that I was a boy myself once. Hurry on, now!"

Holding the rooster under his arm and pinning both wings, Caleb headed up the side of the mountain. I didn't catch up until we reached the ridge. Caleb held one hand over the rooster's eyes.

"What you stealing his sight for?" I asked.

"So he can't find his way back," Caleb answered. "Can't see nothing to fight along the way, either."

I could see red welts on Caleb's arm.

"Rooster do that?" I asked, pointing.

"And only half trying," Caleb answered.

I followed behind trying to catch enough light from the moon to size the rooster up, but the moon had a haze around it making it hard to see much. Finally, Caleb pulled up again.

"We'll go down the ridge here and come out just this side of Echo Creek," he said. "We'll work the lowland and end up at Slaboak Church where we can use the light there to see what I just stole from Elias!"

With visions of fear in my head but curiosity winning out, I followed Caleb down the ridge to the lowland. I envied him all the way—I mean carrying his own rooster! Finally, I saw the light from the church up ahead. The wind was up, swaying the limbs of the big oak in the churchyard and, caught in limb-shadows, the bulb blinked like a lightning bug.

"We'll soon know," I whispered.

"I already know," Caleb said. "I'm just stopping here to show a Doubting Thomas!"

Caleb pulled up under the light, and I took my first good look at the rooster. He was not what I had expected him to be at all. For one thing he was awfully big for a game. He was gray and mottled with black, more like a Dominecker, but I knew that that could have come from a Dom. His comb and waddles had not been trimmed long. They were still scabbed over. Already out of the stag stage, they should have been trimmed earlier.

"Speckled, ain't he," I said, knowing I had to say something about the rooster. I maybe shouldn't have.

"The black spots are straight from old Blackjack," Caleb said. "He's crossed up with a Dom. And this touch of red here is from a Roundhead, just the right mixture!" Caleb looked toward the church. "Nice little church, ain't it?"

I figured that if Mom was right, the next thing Caleb would say was that he ought to be going "regular." Mom said there were generally two occasions when people talked about going to church regular: when everything was going right and when everything was going wrong. Since most of life was an in-between, people ended up just going now and then, something they'd have to pay dearly for one day.

"I really ought to be going regular," Caleb said, fighting to keep the rooster from getting loose.

I swallowed, thinking that Caleb might get us both scorched in the end—borrowing light from a church to see a gamecock! Caleb tucked the rooster tighter, and we headed home.   "How you figuring to get by Mom?" I asked Caleb, knowing that if what he said didn't suit me, he'd be going home alone.

"Been thinking about that for some time now," Caleb answered. "How about telling her I found him along the mountain cold and hungry?"

"He's too fat for that," I answered.

"How about having the rooster fighting it out with a red fox, and my coming along just in time to save him?" Caleb said. "You know how soft-hearted Mom is."

There was no way Caleb was going to fool Mom into thinking the rooster had been fighting with a red fox. Even his trimmed comb and waddles had scabbed over.

"He couldn't come out of a fight looking the way he does," I answered.

"But will after I get through with a handful of pokeberries," Caleb said. "We'll go by way of the creek. Thick as the pokeberries are growing there, they'll be no trouble finding in the dark. I'll stay with the story of the fox."

Following Caleb toward the creek, I was too curious not to go all the way. The rooster was restless. I could hear Caleb: "Ouch, ouch, ouch!"

"I wouldn't let that rooster peck welts on me like that," I said, and hoping to put an end to it, I added, "You could end up with rigor mortis!"

Caleb pulled up.

"Well now," he mocked. "Caught yourself another fancy word, ain't you? Just where did you catch that one?"

Knowing that I had made a fool out of myself before using fancy words on Caleb, I tried to think of a way out. I had caught this one from Nightshade Coulter, who owned the Sourwood Funeral Home in Sourwood, down at Kelsey's, and since Nightshade was always talking scary about bodies laid out, I figured it had to do with something like that.

"From Nightshade Coulter," I answered, and hoped.

Caleb looked at me in disgust.

"If you had listened closer and longer, you would have learned that rigor mortis is the name of a river-town just this side of Louisville; Nightshade has supplies shipped up from there by paddle wheel. I heard him say that."

Knowing I shouldn't have tried it, Caleb being ahead of me in school and all, I followed him now determined not to show my ignorance again. At the creek I could hear Caleb scrapping for pokeberries. I heard the rooster ruffle his feathers and knew that Caleb was rubbing the red juice over him. I caught a glimpse of the rooster. I almost turned my head! The rooster looked like he was just this side of the Pearly Gates, or the gate that a rooster would go through for fighting. We didn't stop again until we were just this side of the house.

"Wish me luck," Caleb said. "I'm going on in with the fox story!"

I stayed behind, and it wasn't Caleb I was wishing the luck on. Being with him made me a part of it all. I waited, quiet as a stump. Finally, I heard Mom say: "Glory be! Glory be!" Knowing that Mom generally said that when she was looking at something pitiful, I sneaked closer. I listened to Caleb's story, so sad that it brought tears to my eyes even knowing the truth of it. Not being able to see Mom, I thought I could see her there shaking her head like something terrible had happened. Finally, I heard her say: "Put him in a box on the porch and place a rock on top so he can't get out, and we'll see about that rooster come morning."

I walked up just in time to hear Mom say as she went through the door: "Shame it couldn't have been a hen you saved!"

Late, I went on to bed and waited for Caleb. I was just this side of sleep when he came. I heard him coming toward the bed. And then I heard it: "Pawk! Pawk!"

I squinted over the side of the bed and saw the big rooster there in the box. Caleb had placed a piece of screenwire over top of it. The rooster quarreled.

"You'll get us both whipped!" I said.

"She won't know unless you tell!" Caleb whispered back. "I'll have him back on the porch come daylight."

Too scared to sleep, I started itching; I always itched when I got real scared. Sometimes I even broke out in a rash, which I had kept from Mom since the day she had rubbed me down with the juice made from boiling pokeberry roots, something I never thought cured the rash but burned it off.

"What's wrong with you!" Caleb whispered.

Mad at Caleb, I whispered: "Probably chicken mites!"

"Well," Caleb said, "you didn't get them from Lightning!"

"Lightning!" I whispered.

"Name of my rooster," Caleb said.

Still mad, I said: "Mom says salt and coal oil mixed will kill mites."

"And leave him smelling like an old lamp!" Caleb whispered, louder than I thought he ought.

But talking did not find us out; the crowing of the rooster did. He crowed just this side of daylight. Mom stood in the doorway with her hands on her hips, a bad sign!

"He was lonesome and hurting, Mom," Caleb said.

"You will be too," Mom said, "off on the mountain cutting wood all day while I'm down here fixing a pot of dumplings! House is probably full of mites by now!"

89

5

Mom told Caleb that he could keep his rooster on the place only until he healed, and then Caleb would have to find a good home for him. Mom was like that: soft-hearted about everything, especially something in need. She was so soft-hearted that she never ate one of her own chickens. She would trade one of hers to a neighbor for one of theirs with the promise that they would keep it until she traded back. She most always traded Prettytom. Caleb and I would take the big Dominecker there and clean the fat hen on our way home with no particulars about it when we saw Mom. Neighbors knew that Mom was good to her word and generally threw in something extra when she traded back, like a jar of her crab apple jelly. Along the river would have meant a trade with Lennie Sanders, but along the foot of the mountain, it meant Ethel Walker. Ethel Walker lived a half-mile around the mountain from us.

"Well," Mom said, "the two of you take Prettytom around to Ethel's and bring a fat hen, dressed, and tell Ethel I'll be back to trade for him later." She looked at Caleb. "Can't keep two roosters on the place without their growing up together and, besides, two roosters is one too many. They'll fight and scare the hens out of laying. That rooster of yours would be no match for Prettytom the shape he's in."

On our way around the mountain, I carried Prettytom and Caleb fussed. He was mad because Lightning hadn't had a chance to have a go at the Dominecker. I knew that Mom's words about the two roosters fighting had smarted. But, holding the struggling rooster under my arm, I couldn't help but think how much the two roosters were alike. A few more black specks, a touch of mottled Gray, and a red spot you might have thought they came from the same brood.

"I'll tell you this," Caleb fussed, "that cull owes a lot to Mom!"

"How come?" I asked.

"Saving his life by trading him off!" Caleb said. "That's how come. I wanted Lightning to have a crack at that rooster. Was already making up a story to tell Mom. Being no fight to it would have given Lightning a chance to build confidence. That's what Elias says you ought to do, give them a cull first!"

But I was thinking how silly it was to be carrying the rooster over to Ethel's in the first place. Mom had traded him off to Ethel so many times that he would have probably gone there on his own.

On our way back Caleb pulled up under a black oak, and we dressed out the hen.

"You know," Caleb said. "You been good about keeping the secret. Could be after he becomes a champion, and I pen him off with some good game hens, I'll give you a rooster of your own out of his brood."

But for some reason I never really thought Caleb would fight his rooster, that he'd end up being too attached and keep him to build dreams on. Thinking out loud, I said: "You really aiming to fight him in the pit?"

Caleb thought about that and shook his head.

"Wouldn't be fair to him if I didn't," he finally said. "That's what he was born to do. Besides, I could use the money."

Later in the evening, I heard Caleb whistling softly to me. It was a bird call we used to get around Mom. It came from Mom's chicken lot. Making sure that Mom could not see me, I sneaked off to where he was. I saw him hunkered down pulling the big rooster back and forth by his tail. The rooster seemed awkward and clumsy. And then Caleb flipped him into the air, and he fell on his side.

"What do you think now?" he asked, grinning.

"I think you'll get us both whipped!" I answered.

Caleb grinned.

"He's took to the hens, too!" I was wondering why Caleb thought that would mean anything to me!

That night in bed, Caleb whispered: "I'm lucky. I mean my life all figured out. Knowing now I was born to fight gamecocks!"

The rooster had taken over his life. What time he wasn't working for Elias Skaggs, he was sneaking to train his rooster. Of the evenings he worked at odd jobs to earn money to place a bet with once he fought his rooster; on weekends he let his money go as payment for the rooster. He never went with me and Mom into Sourwood now for grub. Instead, he stayed home with the freedom to train the rooster. He cautioned me to whistle when we got back near the house and to not eat all the rock candy he knew she would be buying for us.

And one night just this side of sleep, he whispered again: "Yep. When it comes to pretty, it ain't girls at all: it's gamecocks, Lightning in particular!"

I thought Caleb might be right.

6

Maybe it was the bragging on his rooster up at the pit that brought Blinddog our way although I had heard that he could smell roosters a mile off and was always looking for one to handle. He stopped one day while Mom was at Ethel's quilting and Dad was in town buying leather. Caleb stood off watching while Blinddog circled his rooster looking for particulars. Whenever Blinddog wasn't handling a rooster, he was working for Elias. The big man was as scary as a ghost. He wore a black patch over his blind eye, and he had been known to pull the patch down so you could see the socket, which raised the hair on your head. Especially if a boy was around. It was said that the hole where his eyeball had once been was dark and deep with water or something always running from it. I had always turned my head whenever he pulled the patch down; I had enough nightmares as it was.

Caleb watched every move Blinddog made. Finally, too excited to wait, Caleb asked: "What do you think?"

"Better be getting all the money together you can!" Blinddog answered. "That rooster is going to make someone a poke-full!"

Grinning from ear to ear, Caleb asked: "You be willing to handle for me? I'd make it worth your while."

"Be a fool not too," he answered. "And place a little bet on my own. Set your time, but make it quick! Too many people find out about this rooster, and you'll be lucky to get a bet anywhere!" He grinned and looked down at me. "Don't know any widow women needing wood cut, do you?"

"No, but he'll look," Caleb answered for me.

And when Blinddog was out of sight, Caleb said to me: "Nice that Blinddog would want to cut wood for a widow woman, ain't it."

Blinddog had hardly passed out of sight before Caleb started worrying. If it was found out that Blinddog was handling his rooster, he would have a hard time placing a bet. But I had a worry of my own. Blinddog did know roosters. Maybe my problem was that I was not really wanting to believe Caleb's rooster could be that good. I had learned that there was really no way to tell until a rooster was placed in the pit. Strange things often happened. I remembered the night I had watched a five-time winner making a kill, then turning to crow and brag about it. The dying rooster, flopping around with death-quivers, caught the champion by accident with a gaff and pulled him down. They lay there dying together, and bets went out on which rooster would die first. During the early morning hours, the champion lost.

One evening Caleb came home so excited that he coaxed me off on the mountain. The story he told me almost took my breath away. Elias had told him that on the night he chose to fight his rooster that Elias would match a know-nothing himself against him; Caleb would be a cinch to win! A chance to win a bushel of money! The reason being that on sure word there would be strangers at the barn with roosters and plenty of money. They were coming all the way from Lexington and Winchester. Elias would need to match a number of know-nothings to sucker them in on a winner-take-all against old Blackjack! Since he would match against Caleb first, the crowd wouldn't have time to know he was baiting and wouldn't bet against anything he put in the pit. After the first fight, they'd smell it out. But by that time, Caleb would be sitting pretty. Caleb looked humble-like.

"Elias is a good man," he said. "Told me how hard life was for him when he was a boy. That it didn't have to be that way with me." He stared at me. "Don't have to be that way with you, either. Being my brother and all I've decided to cut you in. How much faith you got?"

I fought greed until I was miserable but lost out to it in the end. I shucked out all I had saved. Afraid word might get out on his rooster and that Blinddog would be handling, he figured to scout the next day and place his bet early. Elias held all bet money at the pit, and so we could be sure of our payoff. Elias did this to prevent fights and losers sneaking off before paying their loss. He charged a little for this service, took out for the barn, expenses and all. But with the money we'd have, it wouldn't hurt much.

With Caleb's rooster set to fight on Saturday, I strutted around like a gobbler turkey.

"Think he'll really go after that know-nothing?" I'd coax Caleb to brag.

"Does a bee go after honey?" Caleb would answer.

Knowing the answer to that, I still felt lonesome without my money.

7

On Saturday evening Caleb sneaked the mottled rooster out of the chicken lot, and we were on our way over the mountain. So far our luck seemed to be holding; Mom was at Ethel's quilting. But the going was hard, especially for me. I had to take the lead, brushing weeds and stomping briars out of the way so they wouldn't pick at the rooster. Caleb didn't want to chance a briar catching an eye or the evening dew wetting down his feathers.

We reached the barn early and met Blinddog. He took the Lightning rooster to the back of the barn where he would be penned until he was brought back inside the barn to fight. We shuffled around waiting for the bleachers to fill. Staring inside the pit, my life became miserable. I saw roosters being tossed out for us to pick. I had visions of the big Lightning rooster being tossed our way to be dry-picked. I saw my money flying away like the pigeons that roosted at the barn and flew off at the sound of noise. I stared at Caleb, hoping for hope. He seemed happy enough. But this was his big night, fighting his own rooster! Caleb was a gamecock man!

Time moved as slow as a watched-pot. And then I felt Caleb nudge me with his elbow. He nodded as Mole Burton came through the barn door. Little and wiggly, Mole was said to be so slow that he couldn't carry a thought between two fence posts.

"There's our sucker!" Caleb whispered. "He took the whole bet! I had just made sure he knew I'd be fighting against one of Elias's roosters but didn't know Elias was giving a nothing rooster so that I could win. He wasn't about to bet against Elias. We got ourselves some coal-mine money!"

Knowing that Mole had worked most of his life away inside the belly-mines and probably wasn't up much on roosters, I still worried.

"Don't think he'll forget about making the bet, do you?" I whispered.

"Won't matter," Caleb said. "Elias is holding the money." Finally, I saw Blinddog nod at Caleb and walk out the back door. It seemed like eternity before he came back inside carrying the Lightning rooster. I tried to strike favors on the big rooster while Blinddog carried him toward the pit. Things like trying to believe he was trying to get loose to fight instead of out of the barn. But why wouldn't he be struggling, I thought, with a crowd like this! Who wouldn't be!

This side of the pit I watched Blinddog hunker and fight to fit the rooster with gaffs. For a spare of a moment I felt proud. I mean, I had my money on that rooster; a sure bet! I'd brag down the mountain and hope word did not reach Mom.

I kept waiting for the rooster to show that would be matched against us, the know-nothing that Elias would be bringing through the door as bait. Excitement was just this side of bearable. I thought Caleb's face looked as white as a ghost but thought it was probably the light. He stared toward the rear door, and then we both watched as Elias came through carrying old Blackjack! I could tell that Elias had been drinking heavy. He staggered as he made his way toward the pit. He stopped to grin and spurt a wad of ambeer toward the floor, most of it left hanging on the end of his beard. I swallowed and whispered to Caleb: "Looks like Elias has found him a stranger early with a fat poke and don't want to let him get away! Lightning's fight will probably come after that." And then remembering some gamecock talk I tried to be funny: "Well, the stranger's got to get his craw emptied sometime!"

And then things just happened so fast! I watched Blinddog and Elias step inside the pit, Blinddog carrying Lightning and Elias carrying Blackjack!

"Good golly!" I said. "You're matched against Blackjack!"

Caleb never answered. His eyes were on the mottled rooster, fighting now to get away. He refused to look Blackjack in the eye, something on hindsight I couldn't blame him for. He was putting on a show and bringing the house down. Everything a gamecock ought not do he did. Blinddog dropped him anyway on the sawdust, and Elias grinned and dropped Blackjack. The moment Lightning's feet hit the dust, he set out to make a race of it. He hugged and circled the sides of the pit so fast that he was no more than a blur, around, and around, and around. Blackjack was on his tail feathers, so close at times that he shuffled and knocked feathers loose. But slowing to shuffle, Lightning gained ground. Give credit: Caleb had named him right; he was lightning fast. But who wouldn't be, I thought, with death a short step behind you? The winner, I thought, could end up being the rooster with the most wind. But then I heard a yell from the crowd: "Catch the coward! Wring his neck!"

Elias looked over at Caleb. Tears and ambeer on his face.

"I growed up hard, boy," he said. "Own Mommy even shucked me. No reason you ought to have it any better than I did. I'll wean you tonight just like I was weaned once!"

I saw Blinddog grin, and I knew that he had been a part of it all, too. Even Mole had probably placed that bet for Elias. He would have been the one for Elias to pick.

The crowd yelled louder now. The rules of the pit had been called up. The mottled rooster had lost, if not to Blackjack, then to whoever caught him first. Tears came to my eyes, and through the mist I saw Caleb lean an arm over the side of the pit. His head whirled in a circle, and I knew he was following the roosters. And the next thing I knew, he had snatched old Lightning out of the pit and ran toward the barn door as fast as he could. I wasted no time running after him. I saw Elias throw the black rooster toward us and yell: "Sic 'em!" I heard the crowd laughing. But it wasn't funny. I was remembering that Elias had been the only one who could handle the Blackjack rooster inside the pit; once he made his kill, he was bad to turn on anyone.

Running so hard, before we reached the top of the ridge, I had to stop for breath.

"Not here!" Caleb warned, fighting to hold onto the mottled rooster. "That black devil has still got his gaffs on!"

That made running easier. Hitting low limbs, there was no way to be sure whether the sound was a frightened bird or a shuffling rooster—a big, black one!

"Maybe you ought to drop the rooster and gain time for us!" I yelled at Caleb. "It's probably the rooster he wants anyway!"

"Not yet!" Caleb yelled back.

Caleb never stopped until we were headed over the other side of the mountain. He dropped the Lightning rooster, and we watched him disappear on a dead run into the darkness. I thought for a moment of all the cowards he might be a part of if he lived long enough, but I had a feeling that it would not happen on this mountain; the way he was traveling, it would be in the next county over.

Near the house we stopped for breath. Pulling for air, I said: "We've been shucked clean; Elias has got all the money back he ever paid us for working. We worked all that time for nothing! If he had only tried to fight! Just ended up being a coward, afraid!"

Caleb looked downcast and tired.

"If being a coward is being afraid," Caleb answered, "then I guess we're all cowards at some time or another. But that ain't enough reason to die! I've run from ghosts before."

"I ain't afraid!" I said. "Ain't no coward, either! I was thinking only of the money I had lost now." But I *did* squint around hoping a ghost wasn't close enough to hear.

I was too restless now to sleep, mainly for two reasons: the first being that I had lost all of my money; the second, and running close to first, was that while Elias had been talking to Caleb from inside the pit, Blinddog had grinned at me and pulled the black patch down off his eye socket so quick that it caught me off guard. I had bought myself a nightmare! I hoped Caleb would whisper something to ease my pain, maybe like trying to pay me back. But when he did turn on an elbow and whisper, he said: "How wrong can you be!"

Curious, I answered: "About what?"

"Thinking that a gamecock was the prettiest thing in the world," he answered. "When all the time it was girls!"

But I knew that Caleb was wrong again. The prettiest thing in the world was a hound dog, and I had no money to buy one.

By Way of the Forked Stick

1

Paupered now by Elias Skaggs, and his wants of a gamecock changed back to girls, I guess it was natural for Caleb to turn to the one place where girls went inside, and you didn't have to pay a fare to follow or buy them anything once there: Slaboak Church. Simply put, that's where the girls were every Sunday morning and every Sunday night, and that's where Caleb said he planned to be a "little more regular than before," which I had heard Mom say that most times whenever you heard someone talking about being a little more regular than before, they were generally needing something. Mentioning that to Caleb, he just shook it off. And when I told him that I still wanted a hound dog he said: "Well, the way I see it is that what I want, I can see outright at Slaboak. Since they don't allow dogs of any sorts inside the church, best you can do is pray for one on the inside and hope your prayer is answered on the outside, which is doubtful, your prayer being worldly and greedy."

And so paupered too by Elias Skaggs and my want of a hound dog stronger than ever, I planned to be "a little more regular than before" because I was afraid that Caleb might go on without me and something would happen that I would miss, which was sure to be with Caleb at the end of it.

Caleb chose to go only to the evening services since he said if he was able to sneak one of the girls outside before dark for a long walk back over the hills home, he'd probably end up with little more than knocking briars out of the way for her. A girl wasn't up to much during daylight hours except rolling up her hair, building fires, and cooking. I saw the evenings as offering a better chance of hiding inside the darkness of the mountain if things did not go right.

Going toward Echo Hollow, Slaboak Church was less than two miles from where we lived. It had been built on the front side of Sourwood Creek at the mouth of a narrow hollow known as Dead Mare Branch. A wooden bridge had been built across the creek to furnish a crossing up the short hollow for the handful of people who lived there. Most folks had chosen to build near the mouth of the hollow except for Josh and Todd Bullswick, two brothers who lived together in a one-room log cabin built at the very head of the hollow. Caleb said the two brothers were figured at least three ways by members of the church: those who refused to believe they existed at all, those who believed they had been put there by Satan to tempt them all, and those who used them to point out to the young what Satan would make of you if you didn't follow the ways of the Good Book.

But they did live in a log cabin at the head of Dead Mare Branch, and if you were ever standing on top of the ridge above looking down, especially in the fall of the year when most of the leaves had fallen from the trees, you could see the cabin. Sometimes you could see smoke curling from the chimney, caught by the wind and twisted to a gray snake slithering down the branch which was the path of the wind.

Timbering for a little money during the week, the brothers traveled into Sourwood on weekends and drank up most of what they had made, saving just enough to buy a jug of moonshine to bring up the hollow always during church-time Sunday nights. Traveling from Sourwood by darkness, the first light they came to was the light from the church, and it was here that they stopped to take a measurement on the moonshine inside the jug so that the one not carrying could be sure that the other had not nipped at it along the way. Once they reached the cabin, a measurement could be taken again to see that there had been no cheating going up the branch. But it was their mockery of using church light to measure moonshine whiskey and their arguing and quarreling that could be heard inside the church, often rising above preaching, hymn-singing, and testimonials that many believed in the end would scorch them all—permitting Satan to win.

But, at least to most boys, if and until that day came, there was excitement in thinking that one Sunday night, one or both of the brothers might fall from the bridge into the creek, excitement in imagining the words that were sure to follow, I mean the kind that gets you a whipping by your elders. That's why I had tagged with Caleb and the others on a more "unregular basis" now and then. But let it be.

Caleb said that the church had taken its name because many of the people who went there had slabbed off so many churches. Some believed in washing of feet, some in healing all things by faith alone, some spoke in an unknown tongue and, like Bro. Ross Burdock at Slaboak, some believed in the handling of snakes.

A single light bulb, when not doused by the weather or some boy off the mountain on a bet, burned each night above the front door of the church and was known as the "Sinner's Light," a beacon to guide regulars along the narrow path that led to the church and also sinners and backsliders from off the mountain. Below the light and scribbled across a board that had been tacked there, rested the name of the church and a short message: "Slaboak—Sinners Welcome." Caleb said that the name of the preacher was never put there because the same one never stayed long enough for the paint to dry.

Built mostly from slaboak boards, the bark had peeled long ago, leaving mostly sapwood. Soft and gray-white, the ends of many of the boards had buckled, and the wind from the mountain played under them, singing a sad and mournful song, like lost souls, Caleb said. Worms had pocked the wood, and in the summer, blue lizards played along the boards, their blue bodies sparking the sun. Mud daubers carried mud up from the creek in the back of the church and patched homes in the cracks and knotholes.

Now near winter, when I stood on the ridge looking down, the church looked gray and winter-poor and swayed in the middle like Lottie's old mule, Maud, as scriptured-up as the old mule, but just as bad to backslide and bite when you weren't looking. The church was alone mostly, and lonesome except for rumors and Sundays. The churchyard was shaded by a great black oak, its roots gnarled and heaving out of the earth, building mounds like shallow graves, spooky and ghost-like, a great tree where Sunday nights Caleb stood staring with the older boys, trying to coax one of the girls for a walk home over the mountain—the long way. Some of the boys built nerve to sit inside the church close to the door thinking that would make a sneak-off all right with a girl's mother. Coaxing girls far enough under the shadow of the oak to cheat the "Sinner's Light," boys whispered things too soft to be heard unless you were hiding off close enough. And that, mostly, was why I was going, to cheat both the "Sinner's Light" and the boys and hear what they said, and in between, as sinful as it was, pray for a hound pup. It was mysterious and exciting, exciting because there was always the chance of getting caught by one of the elders of the church—like stealing apples from Lily Patton's apple trees that stood in her backyard in Sourwood, knowing she would law you if she caught you.

The church, as far as we knew, was the only place that hung out a welcome sign for us, too. Where the only fare was a "maybe," a "maybe" that one of us might one Sunday wrestle with the devil and walk inside the church to "come forward," but a "come forward" meant being inside the church instead of outside. Worse still, it meant a trip to the "Glory Hole" later on to have your sins washed away, winter or summer. The Glory Hole was a deep pool of water up Sourwood Creek that had been blessed enough by Bro. Ross Burdock until it was right for baptizing, sanctifizing, and, during winter, freezafizing! The price for a boy being caught meant teasafizing for the rest of his natural life along the mountain.

Excitement for going there was, too, the chance that one of us might get picked off, either caught in sin and conviction, which was unlikely, or tricked there by one of us, which was more likely. Caleb was the best when it came to laying the sign of conviction on someone. So good at it that he had picked a big beech half-way up the mountain toward home where he stopped and cut a notch in the bark for every boy he had had a hand in "bringing forward." He had notched a number of graves there.

Whenever the weather became too cold for us to stay outside, we went inside the church and sat in the pew near the front door and watched. Caleb and the older boys watched the girls, and I usually watched Ned Galloway who sat up in a seat beside the preacher's pulpit chording hymn music for the church on his guitar. Ned lived a hollow over from us and for two years back, in exchange for helping him cut winter wood, he had been teaching me to play the guitar. Ned said I was as good as he was now, but now and then when he looked at me sitting there in the pew, he'd make a fancy run on the strings, and I wasn't sure. Caleb said that Ned was doing that to coax a little more work out of me, that I was already better than Ned. All I knew was if that was so, it was working for Ned; I'd sit there figuring I'd cut a cord of wood to be able to make a run like that.

But inside the church was risky—a preacher lifting the congregation to fever pitch, a keen wind from the mountain sifting through the cracks in the boards enough to water eyes, and the heat from the potbellied stove taking the winter from bugs, causing them to crawl up your britches and make you squirm conviction-like. For almost any movement or show of emotion was the sign that the Spirit was struggling to get inside you, and often needed a helping hand. Tack on that Caleb and some of the older boys were on the side of the Spirit when it came to someone else, and Sunday nights were feared but too exciting to miss. There was always a good chance that someone would get caught except you. That also helped keep me regular.

Caught with signs of the Spirit, you were snatched from the pew, wrestled down the long aisle to the front of the altar, and exposed to the preacher, the congregation, and worse, most of the boys on Sourwood Mountain. Church members now smothered you like a sitting hen. You were gouged, pinched, shouted over, and treated, in general, with the ways to help the Spirit out. A shout from the victim was the best way of telling that the Spirit had made it inside, for everyone knew that when the Spirit struck, you got happy. But with the Glory Hole close on the heels of the Spirit, shouts were generally hard to come by. More so of the winter when the creek was iced over. To catch a cold after being in the water was a sign that the devil had had a harder hold than was thought, and so it was back to the Glory Hole. Copperheads were bad to come off the mountain in the summer to the creek searching for coolness and frogs. Get bit by one, and you were considered too soaked in sin by members like Bro. Ross Burdock to win out!

All in all, the price of "coming forward" was judged too steep to pay. For one thing, you had to give up lying and tobacco right off, and, Caleb said, you could throw in making out with girls, too. While being captured by the Spirit made it easier to get a girl away from her mother, most of the girls wouldn't. Once along the mountain, they had no way of knowing whether you'd be willing to backslide or not, Caleb said. They weren't willing to gamble on a maybe when a sure thing was available.

One Sunday night while I was hid-off in the bushes trying to hear Caleb, who had sneaked a girl away from the "Sinner's Light," I saw the church door open and Rennie Stewart, a gospel woman and church regular, walk out. I watched the sliver of yellow light from inside the church seep through the door and cast off along the mountain. Rennie squinted toward the oak. She'll nab someone, I thought, knowing she had eyes like a cat. But, I wondered why. She had never come outside the church during service before. I thought she was staring toward where Caleb was, and I knew that, caught up with the girl, he would be an easy target. And then Rennie disappeared into the shadows. Poor Caleb, I thought—caught at last! And just when I was thinking there was no way, being so close to him and knowing how bad he was to pull me along with whatever he got into, that I was going to stay and watch them drag him up the aisle, that I'd get me a head start and go back over the mountain alone, I felt a tap on my shoulder and looked up and saw Rennie standing there. She had reached me with the feet of a cat. With visions of my past wrongs coming before me, especially the ones she knew about, and seeing the notch that Caleb would be sure to cut into the bark of the big beech, I thought as old as she was, I might be able to outrun her. But she held me like a fence-stretcher and said: "Hoped I would find you here. You're called inside." My heart sank. "Ned Galloway has had a stroke on his left side. Bedfast, he is. His chording fingers done shriveled up like little bird claws. Says he's taught you good enough for hymn playing." She pinched me hard on my ear. "Lord has provided a way for you to pick and strum some of your sins away! Shame Caleb hasn't learned to play, too! The guitar is inside the church up by the pulpit. Ned says it ain't ever to leave Slaboak, he wills."

Just that quick I had hooked me a job at Slaboak! A job that I found out the following Sunday had pay attached to it. The Sunday after I found out that the amount would depend on who was bringing the message. Bro. Hershel Bates, when he wasn't laid-up with asthma, paid the least; Bro. Minkless Mayhall, with whom Bro. Bates always quarreled, slipped me the most. Finding out about my job, and not being able to go inside the church regular without chance of paying a penalty, Caleb said it was dead wrong and that making a worldly profit from my music inside the church when I ought to be picking for glory was something I'd have to end up paying for later on. Sitting just behind the preacher and seen by all the congregation, I could make as much movement as I wanted and chalk it up to music instead of the Spirit. I could catch all the excitement with nothing attached except my sinful ways. I was riding the strings of a guitar toward a fiery furnace, yet, Caleb saw no wrong in trying to borrow some of the money I made during our trip back over the mountain. Whenever coaxing didn't work, he'd pick briars out of the way saying he wanted to protect my picking thumb, figuring that if coaxing wouldn't get the money, friendliness would.

Often we'd stop at the big beech, and Caleb would cut another notch in the bark, laughing into the wind. While he cut the notch, I thought how it meant more to me now, how I had picked over one of Caleb's friends until my fingers were sore, stretched out there in front of me, refusing to shout and making it hard on everyone, and me so tired that I even thought of ways to help the Spirit along myself.

As we picked our way along the narrow mountain path, I thought of the day that might come when I'd be picking over my own brother, how he'd be more stubborn than all the others but would please them all the most. He'd probably not round-out until daylight. I wondered if he'd give up chewing tobacco whenever he was away from the house and go around telling the truth, mostly. I even thought that he might

not be much fun having around that way. For all of his faults, I liked
Caleb most just the way he was. He was smart and the only brother I
had. Maybe, I ended up thinking, he'll be too smart for anyone to catch.

2

But, finally, in the end, he wasn't—smart enough not to get caught,
that is. He met someone who out-foxed him—a girl! Her name was
Becky Moefield, and she came to Slaboak with her father Jedidiah,
whom Bro. Burdock had invited from Pikeville to hold a revival at
Slaboak. She was as pale and pretty as a night moth, and sang as mournful and pretty as a whippoorwill. She caught the eye of every boy on
Sourwood Mountain, especially Caleb. She joined me the first night of
revival up behind her father and Bro. Mayhall and sang her music to
the background of my guitar. I thought she was almost too pretty to
play for and that I ought to practice more during the day. For some
reason while she sang, her eyes were always on the boys who sat in
the pew near the front door, eyes brown as a buckeye, soft and invit-
ing-like. I noticed little things like that about her—how she would
smile at me, and I'd struggle to keep from missing a chord. For some
reason when her father stepped to the pulpit to deliver the message,
his eyes were on the boys, too, mostly, eyes dark but fiery enough to
scorch a mountain. One thing I thought was certain: there would be
no way to Becky except through him, and with hands swinging high in
the air, hands that looked tough enough to squeeze sap from seasoned
wood, through him didn't seem too likely.

But if I saw that, Caleb didn't. He saw the eyes of Becky Moefield
but tried to dodge the eyes of Bro. Jedidiah. He threw caution to the
wind. Each night now after revival, he'd pull up somewhere along the
mountain and ask: "See the way she looked at me tonight?" And then
he'd leap in the air and click his boots together.

But what I was remembering seeing were the cold, fiery eyes of
Jedidiah and hearing his deep voice calling for louder music. Miss a
chord, I thought, and pay the price, whatever that would be.

"You better watch her pa!" I always answered.

But Caleb would hum and sing as we crossed down the slope, fussing because the church was too stingy to let me bring the guitar to furnish background for his singing:

I got a girl on Sourwood Mountain,
Ho hum a-diddle dum day.
I got a girl on Sourwood Mountain,
Ho hum a-diddle dum day.
So many boys a-hangin' 'round her,
Don't know how I ever found her.
I got a girl on Sourwood Mountain.
Ho hum a-diddle dum day.

My true love's a black-eyed Suzie,
Ho hum a-diddle dum day.
My true love's a black-eyed Suzie,
Ho hum a-diddle dum day.
My true love's a black-eyed Suzie.
Wish she was a little more choosy.
My true love's a black-eyed Suzie,
Ho hum a-diddle dum day.

Ducks in the pond and geese in the ocean,
Ho hum a-diddle dum day.
Ducks in the pond and geese in the ocean,
Ho hum a-diddle dum day.
Ducks in the pond and geese in the ocean.
Devil is a woman if she gets a notion.
I got a gal on Sourwood Mountain,
Ho hum a-diddle dum day.

My true love's a black-eyed Daisy,
Ho hum a-diddle dum day.
My true love's a black-eyed Daisy,
Ho hum a-diddle dum day.
My true love's a black-eyed Daisy.

She'll be mine, or I'll go crazy.
My true love's a black-eyed Daisy,
Ho hum a-diddle dum day.

I got a girl on Sourwood Mountain,
Ho hum a-diddle dum day.
I got a girl on Sourwood Mountain,
Ho hum a-diddle dum day.
One of these days I'll up and take her.
Oh, the pretty things I will make her.
My true love's on Sourwood Mountain,
Ho hum a-diddle dum day.

And we walked the rest of the way home with Caleb thinking of the berry and me thinking of the briar. Caleb whispered things about her in bed—how her father was the sort, he figured, to never allow her to wear make-up or lilac perfume and even to take in a picture show. She was hermited during the day and plucked off the mountain at night like a pretty wildflower and brought to the church to sing sweet hymns. Caleb said nothing about Bro. Burdock setting his eyes on him now. I was afraid of the old man, lived in fear that he might one day find out that I was getting paid sometimes for my music.

And then one night right in the middle of "I'll Fly Away," the congregation at a fever's pitch, I saw Becky drop her eyes on Caleb who had become brazen enough now to move farther up where he would be closer to her. I saw her quickly eye the congregation, probably judge that they were tied up with the Spirit, and wink at him. I missed a chord and hoped that the fever among the congregation would cover me, too. That night along the mountain, Caleb said: "You see her wink at me tonight?"

Lying, I answered: "I saw only what I am supposed to be seeing: the strings of my guitar!"

"Just watch me," Caleb said.

Curious, I asked: "What you planning?"

"Well, the way it is, " Caleb said, "her pa has done cooped her off on the mountain too long. Penned her off from her natural wants until she's wanting even more now. That's the way it is with girls—build a fence around one and she'll fly the coop every time." He stared at me. "Better be planning to walk home alone tomorrow night."

"How come?" I asked.

"I'm planning to ask Becky to walk her home around the mountain," he said. "They're staying with Ross Burdock, you know. Lots of cover between the church and Ross Burdock's. Whoopee!"

Caleb ran down the mountain toward home leaving me to pick my way through the brush alone. I stopped for a moment at the big beech and glanced at the notches there.

At revival the following night, I got to thinking that Caleb could be right about Becky. It was Becky who seemed to be throwing all caution to the wind. She seemed to be singing only to Caleb. I even thought I saw Jedidiah notice the wink she gave Caleb, but he only grinned. Good golly, I thought, Caleb might end up with the prettiest girl in the world. Maybe Jedidiah saw that and figured it had gone too far now to stop.

Walking out of the church after service, Caleb waved me off. I watched him sneak off under the big oak, and I knew he was searching for shadows to cheat the "Sinner's Light." I sneaked around the back side of the tree, searching for shadows to cheat Caleb. Close enough to hear and see Caleb, but close enough also to the mountain to run if Jedidiah came out of the church with Becky.

I didn't have to wait long. Becky came through the door without Jedidiah and stared toward the oak. I watched her walk toward the oak. Caught in light and shadows, I thought she looked even prettier. I thought I ought to take a hitch up on the distance I was from Caleb but was afraid I would be heard. She floated to Caleb like a night moth, pointed, and they walked deeper into the shadows. Caleb stared back toward the church, all clear as far as Jedidiah was concerned. I heard him whisper: "Walk you home tonight?"

I watched Becky stare off. Streaks of moon caught her black hair. She stole a quick look toward the church and whispered: "I want to, but I'm afraid." She moved even closer to Caleb. "Pa won't let me walk with a boy unless he's been "born again." She was close enough now that her breath had to be falling on Caleb's face. "You wouldn't do that so we could, would you?"

Of course he wouldn't, I thought. "Born again" meant "coming forward," and Caleb wasn't about to do that and be kidded off the mountain, but Caleb only shuffled his feet, restless. Becky moved closer.

"How would Pa know if you was to backslide between here and Bro. Burdock's?" she said.

They both giggled.

"You mean a "pretend"? Caleb whispered.

They giggled again.

And then Becky took a step forward, puckered, and kissed Caleb square on the lips.

"If and when we are alone on the mountain is up to you," she said, turning and floating back toward the church.

On our way home Caleb was as silent as the mountain before a storm. I didn't figure he knew that I had been close enough to hear or see, or he would have been saying something about it by now. But I had been close enough to hear the sound of the kiss, excited enough to wonder what it had been like. As I thought about it during the night, I was more than certain that Caleb would have no part of being nailed to the floor just in front of the pulpit. Becky would be gone after revival; the mountain wouldn't. He would never "come forward" on his own! I listened to him snore and wondered how he could drop off to sleep like that after what had happened to him under the big oak. I knew I couldn't. I listened to the night wind, as lonesome and sad as Becky's voice. I heard an owl far off and was glad that he was not closer to the house; that would have been a bad sign. I tried to think of everything except the church, but I saw again things like Effie Price running up and down the church aisle, speaking in an unknown tongue, and I wondered what she had been saying. I thought of Ned Galloway who believed in healing by faith alone and yet was too crippled in his hands to play the guitar again, fingers drawn up like bird claws holding to a limb. And yet as hard as I tried not to let it happen, my thoughts returned again to Caleb. No! Never! Caleb would never make the long journey up the aisle on his own!

But the way it turned out the following night I would never know. Bro. Jedidiah opened service as always: promising a short message and then talking and shouting until his voice was a whisper. After he

110

scorched the rafters, we sang hymns and listened to testimonials. As usual, Rennie was the first, and the longest, to testify. She exposed her own sins and misgivings, both so small that I would have traded with her sure that I would be setting golden traps; and then she exposed ours. That took longer and more heated words. She held her arm above her head and whirled her Bible in a circle which caused some unrest among the congregation since the Bible had gotten away from her a time or two. Plucking the guitar, I added fuel for her fire. I heard the sweet voice of Becky just behind me and wondered if she was staring at Caleb. I glanced up at Jedidiah and saw that he was. I looked down at Caleb. Something was wrong. He was sitting ramrod-straight about center-ways the congregation. He was staring straight ahead, looking at nothing, I thought. And then I saw others staring at him. Ralph Preston, an elder of the church and who was sitting just behind Caleb, had cocked his head and leaned forward. Rennie was still testifying, walking up and down the aisle, looking to see if she had caused a spark to ignite somewhere among the pews. I stared hard at Caleb, looking for signs. And then I saw it—the biggest hornet I had ever seen was sitting square on Caleb's shoulder close to his neck. I knew that it had been stolen from winter by the heat from the stove and had dropped straight down. Caleb had chosen a seat in just the wrong place, but he knew it was there. I could see him move nothing but his eyes toward it. It was trying to crawl but was having a hard time of it on Caleb's starched shirt. One thing I knew: a hornet when aroused would sting. Always! A sting that not even Caleb could bear without showing signs of it. I saw a grin from Don Sutton, who Caleb had notched on the big beech, a grin just short of being under conviction. He knew the hornet had Caleb, and that the night of reckoning could well be at hand, Caleb, the biggest prize of all!

Caleb was as pale as a ghost. I strummed to Rennie's testimony trying to busy myself with something else. And then, caught in Rennie's fire, Chet Thompson, another elder, threw his hymn book into the air. The hymn book opened like the wings of a bird, sailed two pews and landed square on the tip of Caleb's shoulder, and that was that! Aroused, the hornet stung! It was easy to know that—Caleb flinched.

How Caleb was able to not move much, I never knew. Not being able to rub the sting made it next to unbearable. The best I could figure was that the trip down the aisle had to be mighty powerful. But Caleb was losing; I could see that. His face was drawn now in pain and, worse, tears rolled down his face. Rennie, always searching, was the first to see them, the hornet being on the shoulder away from her, she did not see it.

"Glory! Glory!" she wailed. "The Lord has shown me a miracle!"

Her finger was pointing straight at Caleb. Bro. Mayhall leaned toward me and said: "Pick *We Shall Overcome.*"

He nodded at Becky to sing, and I thought she looked like what was happening was all in a day's work. With a chance to get what she had told Caleb she wanted under the big oak, she didn't seem excited now at all.

Excited, I could hardly remember the song even though I must have played it a hundred times. I knew where the hornet had stung Caleb needed itching now. But there was still no movement from Caleb, only tears, more than enough. The congregation moved in on Caleb!

But he didn't come without a struggle, which might have been natural but was a mistake: it only meant the devil was deeper inside him! He grabbed the ends of the pews as he was drug toward the pulpit plucking them like strings of a guitar, holding until his fingers turned white. While they were getting him down there, the elders of the church gathered in a circle in front of the pulpit. Stubborn as a mule, silent as a grave, Caleb was pulled inside the circle at last, so close that I could have touched him with the neck of my guitar. Once there, they wasted no time on Caleb. But still he held out. Bro. Jedidiah said to me with a voice just above a dying fire: "Strum louder, boy! This boy is soaked clean through with sin!"

I strummed until my fingers hurt, like playing at my own brother's funeral! I played until I thought I was almost too tired to go on, got mad at Caleb because he wouldn't shout. Even thought I might help myself if I could have, but then I got to thinking about casting the first stone and had the thought, except for the grace of my guitar, I might be there myself. They patted him, coaxed him, and then got heated by their own words and gouged and slapped him. They screamed and shouted for a miracle, but Caleb's lips were sealed. Once I thought he looked up at me with a look in his eyes that called for help. But what could I do? It hurt me, but a show of tears from me would put me right there with him, catching two brothers in one night—you talk about scorching the church! My only hope was to catch me a "pretend," a "pretend" that I didn't know my own brother, that he was no more to me than one of the others, a stray that had been gathered in.

I was having a time of it myself, being fussed at for not playing loud enough. Caleb was spread-eagled now. Bro. Burdock, trying to spread Caleb's legs ever wider like a pair of scissors, must have touched Caleb in the wrong place with his bony knee. Caleb's scream was pitiful! And that was that: the devil had been cheated out of another soul! The Glory Hole would round it all out!

Outside the church after the service, Caleb waved me off and sneaked under the oak where he had sneaked the night before. I took the same path I had taken also, hitched up and waited. I thought that Caleb had paid a high price for what was to come, but at least he'd be collecting something for the bruises on him, not to count the hornet's sting. If things went right, I thought, he'd end up being the fastest backslider on Sourwood Mountain.

But Becky never showed. Finally, I watched Caleb slip off and turn up the mountain. I walked far behind so that he wouldn't know that I had waited with him.

This side of the big beech I listened for Caleb. Hearing nothing, I knew that he had passed this way and was probably going down the other side the mountain. I walked under the beech and pulled out my Barlow knife, and using the light from the moon, I cut a notch there for Caleb—my own brother.

Sometime during the night I felt Caleb nudge me with an elbow.

"Being my brother and all," he whispered, "I'd like to ask for a couple of favors."

"What's that?" I asked.

"I'd like to borrow a little money to put in the collection plate," he said.

"How come?" I asked.

"If I don't put something in they'll think I ain't rounded out yet, and it's the Glory Hole for me right off!"

That made some sense, and I had a bull-nickel in mind.

Caleb was too quiet.

"What's the other?" I asked, curious.

"You're close to Bro. Mayhall," he said. "See if you can sneak something from him about what it takes to get "churched.""

I wasn't that close, I thought. A mistake and it might be my job and the Glory Hole for me!

3

The next morning while we were on the mountain cutting firewood Caleb leaned on his ax handle and said: "I'll try to hold off the Glory Hole until spring if I don't make out on backsliding or getting 'churched,' but I'll collect from Becky tonight!"

I watched Caleb as he talked. Watched for little things that I had heard came over a person who had "come forward." Like making a new life from an old one. But Caleb looked the same and, squinting down the mountain to see if Mom was out of sight, he took a chew.

"She got tied up inside the church last night," he said.

I wondered how he knew that.

"You won't mind walking home alone?"

"No," I said, thinking that if Becky did show, I'd be sneaking along with them. With Caleb you never knew. He was awfully smart.

That night at revival, Becky's voice went out over the congregation sad and mournful enough, and so did her brown eyes, I thought; but not on Caleb. Caleb, dodging any mention from someone regarding the Glory Hole, kept his head down. He couldn't see that she eyed Lester Gibbs, but Lester could. As the older boys went, he would be a prize only second to Caleb. And before the service had ended, Lester had seen enough to pull under the big oak and wait on the other side of the tree from where Caleb waited. I sneaked to where I could watch both of them.

I watched Becky walk out of the church alone. She floated toward Caleb—or Lester—I couldn't tell at this point. They both looked excited enough although neither knew the other was there; the big trunk of the tree hid them from each other.

Just when it looked like Becky was going to end up with Caleb, she turned and lit beside Lester. He squinted quickly toward the church.

"Walk you home tonight?" he whispered, stuttering—something he did whenever he was excited.

Becky whispered: "I want to, but I'm afraid. Pa won't let me walk with a boy unless he's been "born again.""

I heard a noise from Caleb's side of the tree and saw him sneaking off on the mountain. Knowing that I wouldn't be seeing anything I hadn't already seen, or hearing anything I hadn't already heard, I sneaked off behind him.

I caught up with him before we reached the beech. We walked silent toward it, me afraid that he would see the notch I had cut for him there. And as lowdown as I knew he had to be feeling, goose pimples covered me. But when he reached the beech, he leaned up against it, covering the notches with his backside.

"You saw and heard, didn't you?" he asked.

Knowing now that he knew I was hid off near the oak, I answered, "Yes," ashamed.

Caleb stared off down the mountain. The wind was up now, playing in the trees. Caleb said: "He's a slick old fox!" He even grinned. "Jedidiah."

"How come?" I asked.

"Using Becky to pick boys off the mountain!" Caleb answered. "Me last night, Lester tomorrow night, and who the next night!"

"Good golly," I said. "Good thing you found out. Now you can warn them!"

"You crazy!" Caleb said. "For me it's a way out. With everyone in the same boat, it's all scratched out. All I need do is help the old fox!" Caleb laughed.

"You mean help Jedidiah?" I said, shaking my head.

"You're learning," Caleb said. "Just keep trying to find out what it takes to get churched, and I might come out of this thing clean as a creek gravel."

Maybe Caleb, I thought, but not me. I had troubles of my own now. Coming out of the church door, I had bumped into Bro. Burdock. He had pointed his ninety-seven-year-old finger at me and said: "Prepare, for your time is coming."

And knowing that he believed in the handling of snakes, I'd probably end up with the biggest one of all—worse than facing Jedidiah!

I lay in bed listening to Caleb snore, and trying to get snakes off my mind. I tried to think of things that had come to mean more to me, like money for my trapline. I thought of Bro. Mayhall, how friendly he was toward me, and the money he was sneaking me for my music.

I heard Caleb stop snoring and then felt him touch me with an elbow.

"Don't forget on Bro. Mayhall," he said. "There's got to be a way to get churched.

4

I liked Bro. Mayhall, but didn't think we were close enough for me to go around asking questions about getting churched. I might end up losing my job and getting churched myself. We did have things in common, and maybe that was why he paid for my music. He told me he had spent much of his own life trapping, too, and that he knew traps didn't come cheap. Saying things like he was a boy once himself, his hand sometimes heavy enough on the collection plate to slip me as much as a dollar. He preached powerful and sometimes got happy and kicked his heels behind him, and I had to learn to dodge his boots, but I figured he was the boss, and I had to abide by that. Even his name, Minkless—a nickname that had been tacked on to him up at Elkhorn— probably meant more to me than the others, the excitement and sadness on how it had come about.

Bro. Mayhall had come down from Elkhorn, where he had preached and trapped, because he claimed a Spirit had called him to "come preach regular at the little church beside the big oak." Caleb said that his powerful preaching had caused some in the church to believe he had been called—how else would he have known about the big oak?

But few believed that a Spirit had called him to come preach regular. For the Spirit would have had to cross both Bro. Burdock and Sister Elma to have done that; not many believed a Spirit would. Bro. Burdock had founded the church and gave the land for it; Sister Elma was scriptured-up just this side of Bro. Burdock. Nothing passed at the church without their approval and consent.

On preaching "regular," a Spirit would have had to wrestle with Sister Elma the hardest. Sister Elma was an old maid who kept a younger sister, Dicie, gone most of the time, but dropping in on the church just enough to keep her bed and board. Sister Elma also kept Bro. Hershel, home all the time and preaching now and then whenever he was not down with the asthma. It was Sister Elma's belief that the Lord intended him to preach "regular" at Slaboak whenever his asthma was healed. Caleb said that Dicie ran the mountain like a bitch dog in heat and that Hershel's asthma was nothing more than whiskey, but that sister Elma didn't have to believe that. Caleb said that once you got as much religion as sister Elma had, you had the right to hear what you wanted to hear, smell what you wanted to smell, and if there was a fault to any of these, you had the right to tack it on someone else except your own family. And so Sister Elma claimed that Dicie, when not in church, was off visiting a sick friend, and that Hershel, whenever he was too drunk to preach, was down with asthma that only a trip to the Glory Hole would ease. To get a little spending money, meant staying on the good side of Sister Elma, and he was always willing to go there and earn it. Caleb said that he had been under so many times up there that he could probably tell you the number of crawdads and minnows in the big hole.

Bro. Hershel used the spending money to buy whiskey, and, more than once, some of the boys had helped him home, which was a hard job—mainly because when he was drunk, he was always seeing snakes, and he fought them all the way home. You could be taking him home in the shadows, and fighting brush, and somewhere during his mumbling, he'd yell, "Snake!" and go to thrashing. It was enough to scare you because, although you never suspicioned a snake, you couldn't be sure. He made it sound and seem so real-like. And sometimes after you got him home, too tired to care, Sister Elma would coax you into getting a preacher and helping to get Hershel to the Glory Hole. She claimed that whenever you got down weak, the devil tried to take advantage and that the Glory Hole would take care of that. I didn't know much about Dicie except that I did hear whisperings, and she always came to church painted-up. But I had thought I had smelled whiskey on Bro. Hershel more than once, and I did know that he and Bro. Mayhall argued all the time about who was to preach.

I thought often about Bro. Mayhall's nickname and how sad it had come about. My being a trapper made that so. The name had been tacked on him at Elkhorn because of a mink he had caught and had never been able to brag on after he couldn't show it, a mink that he had caught in a blind-set one night and that was big enough to be a prize winner. The weather had been below zero, and he had taken the mink out of the trap as stiff as a board. I had taken muskrats out of traps that way before. Knowing right off that he had a prize, he stooped to show it off to his little bitch hound, Lucy. She seemed happy about it, too, whimpered and wagged her tail and licked at it. Unknown at the time, she was eyeing the mink for one reason and Bro. Mayhall for another. She was a good hound— winter-poor, but most running hounds are.

Not wanting to chance losing the mink on his way back down the creek, Bro. Mayhall bent its long, slender body into a half-bow and worked it inside his shirt around his back. He figured the heat from his body would thaw it out enough for him to skin once he got it home. With his hair frosted from the cold, and his hands and feet numb, colder than he could ever remember being, he stepped out of the creek just this side of Sam Puckett's General Store, a place, he knew, where old-timers would be sitting around the pot-bellied stove, whittling and telling stories taller than a mountain. Seeing a chance to go inside and tell a story to end all stories, he glanced for his little hound Lucy, didn't see her, but knew she would come in on his trail, and he walked inside.

He figured to slip into his story easy-like, measuring the mink with his arms and hands and watching their eyes open wide. He would watch until the eyes of the old men plainly told him that he had gone too far before he pulled the mink out for the clincher.

Seeing that the time was now, he warmed his hands before the fire and then reached back for the mink. He fumbled inside his shirt. His mouth dropped open. The mink was not there! He felt his shirttail that had fallen out of his britches without his knowing—he had been too cold. The frozen mink had frozen his own hide and had dropped out somewhere along the creek. Turning toward the door, he said: "I'm . . . I'm minkless!"

The old men slapped their knees with the palms of their hands and reared back laughing until they almost fell out of their chairs. And one of them yelled before he closed the door: "Don't feel bad about it, Minkless! You've just told the tallest one yet, and it ain't high noon!"

Knowing that he could be stuck with a nickname like that for the rest of his natural life, he hurried back up the creek to find the mink. He found it all right: small tufts of hair and scattered bones! He found Lucy, too, her belly pooched out and licking her lips.

Caleb said Bro. Mayhall could have come to Sourwood hoping to shed the name, but Bro. Mayhall told me that he had got some used to it. I was more interested in how he had made the set to catch a mink that big. To have made a blind-set was one thing, but even then you had to know the ways of a mink to set it at all. And how did he set it to beat weather that cold? Maybe, I thought, he was as smart on the trapline as he was at Slaboak. At Slaboak he was smart enough to know that the way to the pulpit was through Bro. Burdock and Sister Elma.

He won Bro. Burdock over first. Whenever he was preaching, he pointed his finger at the old man and reminded the congregation that Bro. Burdock was "The Way." The old man was used to show everything right. He doodled enough favors for the old man to winter on. Between dozings, or meditations, Bro. Burdock gloried in it—wallowed in it! Often now, after service and under the limbs of the big oak, the two stopped to talk. Curious, I sneaked to listen one night and wished I hadn't. They talked about improving the church by starting a building-fund drive and ended up talking about snakes. I should have sneaked off then, like you ought to run when you see a ghost, but no one will. On things like that you will stay put when you ought to go and then end up paying the penalty. Maybe it is because one is now and the other later. Bro. Burdock swore that snakes were the only true way to show faith and gain salvation, and Bro. Mayhall agreed with him, said that he had tried them once at Elkhorn, and they had made the difference, right down to who was using aspirins and who wasn't. Bro. Mayhall claimed that his own faith had come by way of a snake. That pleased the old man just this side of the Pearly Gates. Neither said one word about the poor souls who were bit.

After hearing the snake talk, walking home over the mountain was more miserable. The high winds made rattler's tails out of tree limbs. That snakes were supposed to hibernate during cold weather meant nothing to me: I mean, nothing was for certain; I had heard Mom say that!

If there had been any questions left concerning Bro. Burdock's faith in Bro. Mayhall, things like who ought to be preaching regular and the sorts, Bro. Mayhall wiped them out the night he decided to take on Josh and Todd Bulswick and rid the church of that great sin that hung over every member like a cloud: the sin of toleration, as Mom called it. Simply put, Mom said on more than one occasion concerning Josh and Todd's mockery of Slaboak, that according to scripture, the sin of tolerating was the same as doing.

There had been a forewarning that something was going to be different at church services before it actually happened that night. The forewarning had come from Caleb who had a habit of picking up things before they actually happened and, come to think of it, of things that never happened. This time Caleb said that he and Bud Shocky had gone up above Slaboak to take a look at the number of nuts on a butternut tree to see if there would be enough to gather and sell once the frost had set their kernels. On their way home, they had seen Bro. Mayhall working on the bridge by the church that spanned the creek at the mouth of Dead Mare. They had watched from a distance too far away to know exactly what he was doing because if they had gone closer and been seen, they knew he would have forked them over and on their knees for prayer which could have lasted time-wise anywhere between daylight and dark.

But, whatever, Caleb and Bud had spread the rumor enough to guarantee a full house that night at church.

It happened just before the service started. Bro. Mayhall held the church as quiet as a silent prayer. It was so quiet that the snap of the twig, made from the great oak in the churchyard and being used to

120

take measurement on the jug of moonshine Josh and Todd were taking up Dead Mare, cracked like a rifle inside the church. And then came the low quarreling from Josh and Todd, and everyone inside the church knew exactly where they were: standing on the church-side of the bridge that led up Dead Mare and using the "Sinner's Light" to see where the moonshine mark was on the twig. The congregation seemed too mortified to move, and Bro. Mayhall had no intentions of letting them off easy.

"And what might that be?" he coaxed.

And even though everyone there knew that Bro. Mayhall had heard the same thing more than once with the rest of them, they hung as silent as a spider's web. Bro. Mayhall looked out over the congregation at everyone except Bro. Burdock but found no one willing to lock eyes with him. He coaxed: "Sister Elma?"

Without looking up she said, almost in a whisper, but to a congregation so quiet that even a whisper this night sounded like a raised voice: "Could it be the wind in the big oak, Bro. Mayhall?" she said.

And then the quarreling outside became louder: "Damn you, Todd! I'm being cheated by a green twig and a slanted light, and I know it!"

"Hear me!" Bro. Mayhall thundered. "The salvation of Slaboak is as stagnant as a summer creek! To permit is as sinful as to do! If there be among you any who doubt my calling to Slaboak to preach "regular," let them watch now!" He looked down toward Lottie. "Testify Sister Lottie while I ease out the back door to wrestle with Satan!"

While Bro. Mayhall eased out the back door, I saw Caleb and some of the boys with him along the pew slip out the front door. Sitting beside the pulpit cradling the guitar, I couldn't leave without being seen. And with Lottie testifying, I knew that I couldn't hear whatever happened outside. On her second trip around the room, she said to me: "A little hymn music to go with the testimony if you don't mind, honey!"

"If you don't mind?" What choice did I have? And so I strummed away, knowing that whatever took place outside would have to come by way of Caleb. But, then, I had learned in time that often things coming that way were even better than the path they had actually taken—always too good not to believe.

And so that night on our way home back across the mountain this is what I never saw:

Bro. Mayhall caught up with Josh and Todd at the edge of the bridge. He could see them plainly here for they would not be out of the rim of the "Sinners Light" until they were nearly halfway across the bridge. He watched the jug of moonshine swinging back and forth in Josh's hand.

"What would you do if Judgment Day was to come, and you was a-standing here at the beginning of this bridge with that jug of whiskey in your hand?" Bro. Mayhall thundered out to Josh.

Josh staggered around like an uneasy horse (or mule) and sorta scratched his head like he would plow out his answer from inside. And then he drew up his lower lip and a grin came to his face.

"Why, I reckon I'd just ease this here jug over to Todd, preacher," he answered. "And then just sit back and let ol' Todd worry about what to do."

"Poor, wretched soul that you are!" Bro. Mayhall said. And then he raked his finger under Josh's nose, drew Josh's eyes to the finger and led them to sight in on a large dead oak that the moon outlined along the bluff on the right side of the hollow. "Mark me!" he said. "Mark me! Doom is on the two of you. And some night soon a big ball of fire is a-going to roll down from that oak! Maybe it will come from the left of it, maybe from the right of it. Maybe straight through it! Whichever, it'll leave you two a burning cinder here at the bridge, most likely!"

Josh stared at the dead oak. He pulled the cork from the jug, took a swig, and with the juice running down his chin he said: "Reckon I believe what only I can see."

"So do I," Todd said. "And right now I reckon to take measurement on that jug to see how much is left after a pull like that. 'Pears I got me a witness tonight."

"Beware of the ball of fire!" Bro. Mayhall shouted. "Prepare!"

His fiery eyes must have unsettled Josh, for he hit the jug again before Todd could take a measurement. And then Josh and Todd quarreled their way across the bridge and up the hollow. Bro. Mayhall returned to the church, and to the disappointment of the congregation, didn't appear to have wrestled or changed anything outside.

But on the following Sunday night, he stood at the pulpit with his head cocked toward the window, as silent as midnight. He never had to keep it cocked long. The snap of the twig and the quarreling drifted among us. Bro. Mayhall looked out over the congregation.

"Testify, Sister Elma!" he boomed out, as he eased toward the rear door. Again, Caleb and the other boys had followed.

With the measurement taken at the "Sinner's Light," Josh and Todd turned toward the bridge. Josh was in the lead and Todd, as usual, was a few feet behind.

Josh might have made it across the bridge; I mean, you can't ever be sure about that, staggering and all. But, truth was, he never followed his usual pattern, which was to take the right side of the bridge. Trees were closer there and offered more shadows. But this night, he stopped to stare toward the dead oak high on the bluff and, maybe shying from it, he crossed from the left. I mean he started to cross. He ended up hitting a loose log (the spot where Caleb and Bud had seen Bro. Mayhall working that day), and a hole sucked him down. A low moan drifted back up through the hole.

Now a moan from Josh had come to mean one thing to Todd: that Josh had probably hit the jug. It generally came at the end of a long pull.

"Josh? Josh?" Todd quarreled. "Hold up. I heard that! Time for a measurement. Slow up now. You're a-walking too fast!"

"Todd?" Josh hollered back up through the hole. "The thing is, I ain't a-walking at all! I'm down here flat of my back!"

"Down where?" Todd asked, swaying on the bridge. "Where are you, Josh? Come out from the shadows!"

Josh hollered back up: "Shadows you say, Todd? I've fell through the bridge!"

Not being able to steady himself bending over, Todd opened up like a pair of scissors and landed on his rump. He leaned over and peeped down through the hole.

"Mighty funny thing to me," he said. "I've knowed you to cross this bridge tight as a mash-fed crow, and you never fell before! Now I got me a measurement on that jug, Josh. You just come on back up here on top the bridge. Won't do you no good down there!"

"Forget the jug, Todd," Josh yelled back. "Help me. I'm soaking wet!"

"Wet!" Todd said. "You've busted the jug, you crazy fool! Is it all the way busted? I mean, can you feel it?"

"Only thing I can rightly feel," Josh answered, "is the cold, cold water of the creek. Give me a hand!"

"If you can't feel the jug, can you see it?" Todd asked.

Josh answered back this time, but in a quivering voice: "Todd! Todd! My own dear brother. I think my eyes is done both gone out. All I see is darkness!"

Todd folded his arms over his chest and drew up his lower lip to scold.

"You had the jug with you when you went over," he said, "and if you can't come back with it, you'll come back with your own help!"

And then something moved along the rafters of the bridge. Josh jerked his head at the noise. The noise came from the right side of the bridge, the direction of the dead oak.

"That you, Todd?" Josh asked, in a low, soft voice, his eyes searching the darkness. "That you, my dear old brother Todd, coming to help me out of the mud?"

Bro. Mayhall moved slowly along the rafters of the bridge. Steadying himself, he pulled a flashlight from his coat pocket and covered the globe with a red bandanna. He threw the red beam of the light first along the bluff of the hill, crawled it down the slope and under the bridge, and crossed Josh's half-mud-filled eyes with it.

"Todd!" Josh yelled. "I can see it, Todd!"

"Is it busted?" Todd yelled back down, bobbing his head in a half-doze.

"Is what busted? " Josh yelled back down.

"The jug, you drunken fool!" Todd said.

And, maybe thinking that he was pinned in the mud on Judgment Day, Josh set out to make amends. He set out—making it was another matter!

"My dear old brother, Todd," he answered back, "I don't believe I know what sort of jug you're a-talking about!"

"Danged if you ain't drunk it all!" Todd said. "Has the shine made you that crazy?"

"Old dear, old brother, Todd," Josh answered back, "say you are only kidding. Say that you know that your dear old brother would never touch a sip of foul moonshine!"

"I hope you get caught in a washout!" Todd said.

The red beam of light crossed Josh's eyes again.

"Oh, Lord, Todd!" Josh said. "It's that ball of fire from the big dead oak!"

Bro. Mayhall curled his lips and sent a low moan to rattle among the rafters.

"I hear 'em!" Josh said. "I hear 'em a-coming, Todd. They're creeping up on me and me stuck tight here in the mud. Help me, Todd!"

"You're tight all right," Todd said, lifting the stick that he had taken the last measurement on toward the light.

Looking around like a thief in a corn patch, Josh cupped his hand to one side of his mouth and whispered back up through the hole.

"Blast you, Todd!" Josh said, easy-like. "You'll get me burned to a cinder over that jug of moonshine!" He raised his voice. "Say you are only kidding, Todd. Tell 'em, Todd!"

Scooting along the bridge to get a better look, Todd reached the hole and lost a leg through it. His brogan brushed Bro. Mayhall's face. Bro. Mayhall clamped down on Todd's leg. Todd kicked with all his might.

"Josh!" he screamed. "Let go, you drunken fool. Loose my leg! I can't pull you up!"

"Oh dear, old brother, Todd," Josh said, "how could your dear old brother Josh have hold of your leg when he's stuck down here in the mud?" And then he cupped his hand to one side of his mouth like he was trying to hide the sound of his voice. "The dead oak, Todd!" His voice was next to a whisper. "The dead oak on the bluff. Balls of fire! Be careful what you say, you drunken fool, or you'll get us both burned to a cinder!"

Todd looked off toward the dead oak on the bluff. The red moon was bright, and maybe it blurred Todd's sight. He lost his balance, and his long nose slid between the cracks of the logs. The red beam of the flashlight crossed his eyes.

Trying to stagger back up, he stopped to whisper down: "Did you strike a match, Josh! Tell me you struck a match to look for the moonshine!"

"How in Heaven's name dear old brother Todd, that is, tell me dear old brother Todd, that is, pray tell me dear old brother Todd, how you think your decent-living brother could strike a match when I am wet up to my ears?" He cupped his hand to one side of his mouth again and whispered: "You poor drunken fool that you are! You'll get us both scorched!" And then before he could say more, the beam of light crossed his eyes again. His voice started like a low wail and gained strength as it climbed. "It's balls of fire!"

Todd fell again, and this time Bro. Mayhall reached out and pinched his fingers on Todd's nose.

"Josh!" Todd said. "Where might your hands be?"

"Down here, dear old teetotaler brother," Josh answered.

"Yeooooooooo!" Todd screamed. "It's got me, Josh!"

"Hush, you drunken fool!" Josh said. "You're a-scaring me to death!"

Todd rolled over on his back, and Bro. Mayhall struck a country match and held it through a crack just right to hit Todd on the seat of the pants.

"Whoops!" Todd yelled. "It's balls of fire!"

Josh came out of the mud like a wild man, shinnied up a ten-foot bank and didn't stop until he was inside the church. Todd was a close second. Mayhall came in last.

Sister Elma was going strong, and when she saw Josh and Todd come in and take a front pew, she was next to setting the church on fire with her testimonial. Like with the two of them inside the church, a great weight had been lifted. Bro. Mayhall eyed her strongly.

"Amen, Sister Elma!" Mayhall said. "You can testify your way out as well as in. Circle the room no more!"

Bro. Mayhall eyed Josh and Todd. He said nothing, just stared, his eyes like burning cinders. Todd squirmed, uneasy, and looked awfully pitiful. He wrung his hands and licked his lips. Josh kept his eyes on the floor, and then he reached inside his pocket, pulled out a green twig, and handed it to Bro. Mayhall. And then he puckered his mouth and said: "Hal . . . hal . . . hallelujah!"

"A . . . a . . . amen!" Josh said.

"Amen!" Bro. Mayhall said, and then the "Amens" echoed the church. Mayhall raised his hand for quietness and got it without any trouble at all. He said: "It matters not how you gather, but only that the strays are in the church! Music, boy!"

Taken in by the miracle Bro. Mayhall had been given the power to perform, Bro. Burdock suggested that the congregation start a building fund to expand the church and tack on a special room for their "regular" preacher—mainly Bro. Mayhall.

Bro. Mayhall had wasted no time taking Bro. Burdock's suggestion on setting up the building fund. He even told the congregation that he was putting most of his own salary in the pot, that now that trapping season was in, he would return to the trapline for awhile and earn his keep, reminding the congregation that the Apostle Paul had done that— that while the Apostle Paul had earned his keep by making tents, he would earn his by setting traps. The congregation liked that; I didn't. With two on the creek, I stood to catch fewer varmints.

Until Bro. Mayhall took to the trapline, I never really knew how fewer. And yet the signs were there. But, so was Bro. Mayhall. Early of the mornings when I ran my trapline, I always met him coming back down the creek, making his way through pokeberry stalks, elderberry bushes, and patches of buckberries. He was always carrying a nice catch of muskrats and sometimes a fat possum. With me maybe holding an unprimed kit or two, he would stop, talk, and stare at my meager catch.

"How's it going?" he always asked.

"Not good," I'd answer, trembling from the cold.

"Man's catch is as good as his faith," he answered. "You're being watched, boy!"

And then one morning as he walked off, I thought to myself: *And*

127

so will you be watched, but not by a Spirit. But I knew that if he was taking varmints from my traps, catching him might be like chasing a Spirit. Finding his boot prints along the creek was easy. The trouble was, they were always high on the bank. Wherever I had made a set, his prints were nowhere to be seen. If he went to them, he went by way of water where the current would steal all signs.

By seeing his footprints high on the bank I learned one thing: if I found prints near a trap, I would know whether it was Mayhall or not. There was a chip out of the right heel of his boot as large as a quarter.

I knew that if he was stealing my rats, he wouldn't find it hard to do. A trapper knew the ways of a trapper, the ways of the varmints. He knew where the good sets would be by watching signs. And there were only so many good sets along any creek.

When I was just this side of thinking no one was running my line ahead of me, that I was having a winter of bad luck, I caught me a sign: the tracks of two boots in the soft mud by one of my sets! One of the boot tracks had a chip in the heel as large as a quarter. Bro. Mayhall had been careless.

One Sunday night I watched Bro. Mayhall get happy, leap to click his heels together, and I saw the chip from his boot again. Now I knew for sure, I thought, as I plucked the strings of the guitar. But know what to do about it, I didn't. I thought I might start by adding up how much he was giving me out of the collection plate and how much I thought he might be getting out of my traps. At least that would give me time to think, and then I could figure on a way to keep the better of the two.

That night after we had gone to bed Caleb asked me again: "Haven't got around to asking Mayhall anything about getting churched yet, have you?"

"Not yet," I answered, knowing that I never would but keeping Caleb close in case I had to ask his help about Bro. Mayhall stealing my muskrats, a fat possum now and then, and maybe even a mink that he was not showing. Probably giving me money from the church to buy traps so that I could catch more varmints for him! Not really paying for my music at all. And what little I got from Bro. Hershel the few times he preached was probably for not saying anything about the whiskey on his breath. He preached up close to my music—so close that a struck match might have singed us both. Caleb said whiskey fumes would blow touched to fire.

5

It wouldn't be easy to do anything where Bro. Mayhall was concerned. While Caleb said that Mayhall had a roving eye and judged him a short-timer, I couldn't see why he would ever want to leave Slaboak. He was preaching "regular" now except for turning the pulpit over to Bro. Hershel just often enough to pacify Sister Elma, always bragging when he did so that Bro. Hershel's message was God-sent. He would end up asking the congregation to join him in a silent prayer asking for a cure for Bro. Hershel's asthma. Caleb said he would have given a pretty penny to know what Mayhall was really praying for during the silence, that he had to be smart enough to know that Hershel's problem would take care of itself. Bro. Hershel wouldn't give up whiskey and that was that. All Mayhall had to do was bide time.

And, all in all, I wasn't faring too badly. Bro. Mayhall had increased the pay for my music, and I bought less traps. With the coldest of winter on us now, my traps couldn't be taking much, even for Bro. Mayhall. Also, catching up on baptizings from the revival, I was making extra money. The Glory Hole paid well. Caleb said that was because the fever was always higher there, that the ones who came out of the water were happier, either because of the Spirit or being shed of the ice, and that the ones who saw them go in, thinking they never would, gave more in appreciation—and bet more on how long before he backslid. But, Caleb could talk now. While he had been there many times before to watch, he wasn't going there now. And when he had gone, he had been able to choose his weather. He was afraid to go now, no matter the weather, afraid that he would be snatched from the bank and held under the ice while his nose was pinched together. It was hard work, going there, a long way up the creek and seemed farther back down. And the colder the weather, and the icier the water, the better to test faith! Catch cold and you caught it from Bro. Burdock.

A baptizing was no baptizing without music: so said Sister Elma, and so agreed Bro. Burdock. I strummed the guitar there with fingers so cold that they froze to the neck of the guitar like bird claws. And whenever Caleb heard me complain, he told me that was what happened to poor Fred Gallup, why he had had to give up playing music at the church—his bony fingers eat up with arthritis from the cold. I'd probably end up the same except a little worse since I was taking money from the church. He said nothing about the money I loaned him from the collection plate that he spent at the picture show: church money! On girls, too!

The trip to the Glory Hole was work enough. We started at the church and picked our way along a narrow path that led upcreek, fighting for footing on the frozen land and dodging weeds winter-killed and hanging over the path. And Sister Elma, who couldn't carry a tune in a rain barrel, was always off-key, making it hard for me to strike the right chords. She called for music all the way, up and back. Trying to play the guitar and keep my eyes on the narrow path was hard. In places, the path wound so close to the creek that a slip meant going in the water. And at times when I did slip, catching myself just before going in, Bro. Mayhall would grin at me and say: "Make it all the way, and I'll baptize you on the spot!"

The Glory Hole itself had been gouged out of a high mud bank far enough to catch and hold water, and it remained at least five feet deep year round. A huge sycamore hovered on one side of the hole, and its gnarled roots stretched nearly half-way across the hole. Wherever the roots stuck far enough above the water, people gathered and used them for seats during baptizings, especially Bro. Ross Burdock. I was certain no mink had ever traveled the creek without searching under the roots. It was the best of mink sets, but also, for me, the worst. There was no way I could set a trap under the roots. With my luck Bro. Burdock, his tiny feet dangling below the roots, would end up hitting the spoon of my trap, which would jump and snatch him ankle-high. Trapping for me would have been over then! I was sure, the way it was with me now, there would be no trapping where I'd be going. You never knew which root he would choose.

Once at the Glory Hole, Bro. Mayhall would break ice and wade in, the weather so cold that the ice knitted back together behind him. The sinner was coaxed in, pinched by the nape of the neck with one hand while his nose was pinched by the other, and he was pushed under the water, ice forming above him. Sometimes Bro. Mayhall held them under for so long that the congregation squirmed, but they always popped back like a fishing cork and made their way to the bank, mouth open and hair frozen. Perched on the root of the sycamore, Bro. Burdock "Amened" above the others, his short legs dangling below, reminding me how smart I was not to have set a trap there. I was afraid enough of the old man the way it was.

To believe that the Glory Hole was healing water, Caleb said, was plain silly, blessed and made so by Bro. Burdock or not—that he had swam the most of one summer up there and couldn't even get a stubbed toe healed. Besides, Caleb said, take Bro. Hershel Bates: as many times as he had been under up there, he would have been the healthiest man on Sourwood Mountain. Of course, he seemed better when he came out of the water: he was sobered up, or next to, but it wouldn't stick. Generally, though, sobered enough that he stopped seeing snakes. Of course, too, Sister Elma had the right to believe about the hole whatever she chose, and what she chose was to take Bro. Hershel there every time he got on a bad drunk, or, as Sister Elma had the right to believe, an asthma attack.

The trouble with Hershel was that he never had an attack at a decent hour. His attacks generally came at night, and the trip to the Glory Hole often included only Bro. Mayhall, Bro. Hershel, Sister Elma, and me. She again demanded music all the way up and back. Under the light of the moon and stars, off we went. Because of Sister Elma's age and Hershel's condition, the going was slow. We picked our way by moonbeams along the narrow path. Listening to Sister Elma sing was bad enough; cold, her voice was as squeaky as a well pump. But I went for the greed of money; I figured Bro. Mayhall went for the sole right to preach regular. Bro. Hershel went, Caleb said, because as drunk as he was, he knew it was the only way he could get more money from Sister Elma; Sister Elma went because she had the right to believe it would help his asthma and was sure it would make it easier for her to get some sleep when they got home. If going had been tough, coming

131

back was harder, especially after we got back to the church, and I went home alone. It was a long and spooky trip. Bro. Mayhall's fiery words at the Glory Hole traveled with me. Briars snatched at me like the tines of the devil's fork; the red moon was his fiery head; the winter wind, his voice, and the change that Bro. Mayhall had slipped me rattled like the thirty pieces of silver!

6

It was the coldest night of winter that Bro. Mayhall came to the house to ask if I could come to the Glory Hole and furnish music because Sister Elma had asked for it. Mom answered the door, and she tried to tuck her shawl around her to ward off the cold that came through the door. Bro. Mayhall said that Bro. Hershel had come down with his worst attack, and that Sister Elma was in a bad way with worry.

"Be a cold trip for a boy out tonight," Mom said to Bro. Mayhall.

Bro. Mayhall nodded in agreement and slapped his hands together for warmth. He looked at Mom.

"Could be a death-wish this time!" he said.

"Better go then," Mom said. "Bundle up and stay high on the bank."

We found Bro. Hershel slumped over in a chair at Sister Elma's. Sister Elma stood close by, wringing her hands. Whenever she would speak to Hershel, he would flail the air, act sulky, and then pull for air. I caught a whiff of his breath and wondered just how close you had to be to scripture not to smell that!

The weather was even more raw by the time we got him up, quarreling and speaking in an unknown tongue, and on his way. A light skim of snow covered the land, and the creek was white and frozen solid. Now and then Hershel would fall, and Sister Elma, maybe figuring that he had chosen to die there, would scream and wail, or he would yell, "Snakes!" which scared Sister Elma and caused her to crowd me on the path. Caleb had told me that Sister Elma lived in fear of snakes, the worst he ever saw, feared them more than the Devil. By the time we reached the Glory Hole, Hershel was barely standing on his feet.

His talk was a mumble, and he was flailing the air something fierce, even striking at Bro. Mayhall.

Bro. Mayhall wasted no time. He broke the ice by pounding the heel of a boot against it and waded in, breaking a path through the ice. I eased over to the sycamore and found a root where the trunk of the tree would break the cold wind that came out of the hollow. I watched the ice knit back over the path that Bro. Mayhall had taken. Trembling from the cold, he looked up at Hershel and Sister Elma, and then he looked over at me.

"Music!" he said.

My fingers were frozen, so cold that I could have plucked a sycamore root and never known the difference. My music broke the silence, and I stared at Sister Elma who was trying to keep Hershel from falling. With a deeper shiver to his voice, Bro. Mayhall said: "Coax him in, Sister Elma!"

She tried but couldn't. The spirit Hershel was fighting now was probably better than a hundred proof!

With a heavier voice Bro. Mayhall said: "Get thee behind him, Sister Elma. Let the slick and frozen bank do God's work!"

Sister Elma leaned toward the cold water.

"Oughten he come on his own, Bro. Mayhall?" she asked.

With a still deeper voice Bro. Mayhall said: "Get thee behind him, Sister, before I get froze in and can't get out!"

She didn't really. She jumped at Bro. Mayhall's rough voice, slipped, and grabbed Hershel for support. She ended up flipping him in the water like a bullfrog jumping off the bank. She landed on her rump and hurried back to her feet. And by the time she was steady again, Bro. Mayhall had pinned Hershel by the nape of the neck. He gave a jerk, and Hershel went skidding over the ice past him, ending up at the roots of the sycamore, where he broke through. Bro. Mayhall reached and pulled him out, but as he did so, I saw that Bro. Hershel had also pulled a slender root out with his other hand. Slender and water-soaked, the root was as limber as a piece of string. Still holding the root, he fought for the bank where Sister Elma stood. Thrashing the water with the root, he wailed: "Snake, Snake!"

Bro. Hershel flung the root toward Sister Elma. She screamed, lifted her dress, and danced a jig! Bro. Mayhall was watching.

"Sister Elma!" he scolded.

Sister Elma looked like she had swallowed something, but she still squinted like she was trying to find the root and be sure. Bro. Hershel, still in the water, was holding to the bank, moaning. Bro. Mayhall stood over him.

"How does he look, Bro. Mayhall?" Sister Elma asked.

Bro. Mayhall looked down at Hershel. He was flopping in the water like a fish pulled to bank.

"Might make it this time and might not!" Bro. Mayhall said. "This could well be my last trip up here with him!"

I figured that Bro. Mayhall was tired of pretending and coming out on cold nights. I know I was.

Hershel had gone quiet. Finally, he stared toward Sister Elma and said: "It ain't always been asthma, Sister!"

Sister Elma looked around as if someone else had come with us. She leaned toward Hershel.

"Hush!" she scolded. "Who's to know!"

"Sister!" Bro. Mayhall scolded. "The One that marks the fall of the sparrow surely couldn't miss something as big as Hershel!"

"Shall we pray?" Sister Elma asked.

"Pray for the jig you danced!" Bro. Mayhall said. "Your faith lost to a snake! Leave Hershel to me."

He jerked Hershel to his feet, kicked him in the rear-end. Hershel scratched his way to the top of the bank. He shook the cold water from him like a wet dog.

"Oughten we at least pray for him?" Sister Elma said. "We ought to do something!"

"And that something," Bro. Mayhall said, "is to quit giving him money. With what he's got inside him, he'll probably be the only one of us to not come down with something!"

We turned now toward home, Hershel much steadier on his feet. Bro. Mayhall stopped, handed me a frozen dollar and whispered: "Leave what you saw tonight between me and you."

With the frozen greenback, he gave me already thawed out in my pocket, and with thoughts of more to come, I figured I could probably keep the secret.

Farther along, Sister Elma looked down at me and said: "A little music would help."

I stared up at her. Once, I might have strummed my fingers red if she had said that to me. But this night I had watched her dance the jig to the snake-root, too scriptured-up to know that a snake didn't come out during the winter.

"Too cold for that!" I said.

She smiled and whispered back: "'Tis cold ain't it, honey."

And, walking home, I got to thinking about a winter snake. How scripture-heavy could be a dangerous thing, or, could it? If the Spirit could catch a sin unseen, couldn't It also coax a snake out in the dead of winter? I'd watch the brush just in case. I was probably heavier in sin than Hershel; I knew Caleb was.

7

With Sister Elma and Hershel out of the way now, Bro. Mayhall showered all his attention on Ross Burdock. I would have rather gone back to the old way. For he called on the old man now more often to come to the pulpit and "light the fire," and light it he did, with most of the heat, I thought, catching me. Caleb, knowing that I had a fear of the old man, made it even worse. I thought that Caleb was mad at the world now and was taking part of his madness out on me. He was always complaining when we went home over the mountain—how hard it was to find girls who would even talk with him before or after church. They were afraid that he was still under conviction, he said, and wanted little truck with him, and that the rumor about being under conviction was being helped along by his own friends. He said that just like he had never been a part of any problems they had had even though he had heard Mom tell us a hundred times that birds always come home to roost. It was as if I were the one who coaxed the hornet down on him. I had had to play music over him; he knew that. I would have lost my job, something he was forever reminding me about: thinking more of a job than my own brother!

Every time now that Bro. Burdock took the pulpit, Caleb said he noticed little things; mainly, that the old man seemed to stare down at me more than usual. Caleb said that he figured the old man knew I was picking for money instead of glory. My fear of him became even greater, and with reason enough. Bro. Ross Burdock! Founder of the Church. Ninety-seven years old and had never taken an aspirin! Old and wrinkled as a winter apple, a shock of hair white as snow, but cold, black eyes that caught the thin light and sent out sparks! It was a mystery how a man so small could hold so much lightning. I knew that he believed in the handling of snakes, and I had made the mistake of telling Caleb about what I had heard under the oak that night. I never could keep a secret for long. If snakes came, Caleb said, I'd probably go first because of the money I'd taken. He said nothing of having to go with me for the money he had borrowed. I watched the old man closely. Watched him preach thunder and dance around on birdie legs, and I thought of snakes. And sometimes he'd burn me with his eyes: "Pick for glory!" he'd say to me.

And on our way back over the mountain, Caleb would say: "Better keep an eye on that old man; he knows!"

One night on our way home, Caleb pulled up under the beech and said: "I wouldn't be expecting help from Mayhall if I was you; he's a short-timer. I wish you'd ask him about getting churched. You might not be as close to the next one."

But figuring that Caleb was just mad because I hadn't loaned him all the money he wanted, I paid little attention to what he said about Bro. Mayhall. I should have paid more attention.

Two Sundays later Bro. Mayhall was gone, taking with him all the money from the building fund and Dicie Bates!

"Money is one thing," Caleb said. "Dicie is another. He'll never hold that woman!"

"How come?" I asked, curious.

"She's as slick as a river eel and just as loose," Caleb said. "Once the church money is gone, she'll latch on to another carp!"

The following Sunday, Bro. Burdock took the pulpit. His great shock of white hair danced to the stomp of his foot while his ninety-seven-year-old finger pointed out over the congregation, resting for a moment on everyone. He spoke of aspirins, lust, and all our other misgivings. The time had come to set things right with the church. Things would be set right—he promised us that!

On Tuesday Caleb picked up word that the old man had gone to a revival over on Blaine, that he had gone to have a meeting there with the preacher holding the revival. His name was Mordecai Tate, a circuit rider who was supposed to be working miracles on that side of the mountain. Brimstone was his nickname, given because of the power of his message and the way he delivered it.

By Saturday we learned that Bro. Brimstone would be visiting Slaboak after the revival ended there on Sunday, a week away!

On Sunday Bro. Burdock took the pulpit again and verified all rumors that had come ahead of him. If Slaboak was to stand, he said, there must be a flushing-out! Bro. Brimstone would be with us the following Sunday to start the flushing. Tears streamed down the old man's face as he said he wanted to see the church set right before his passing on. Well, first off, it shocked everyone to hear Bro. Burdock speak of passing on. I guess we never really thought of the old man going like that, the way we would go. Most figured he'd probably pick the time and the place, that he'd just one day ease off along the mountain and lift like a little bird and disappear into the clouds. Surely, Bro. Burdock would not go any other way!

While he talked of death and short-time, I watched him closely. Under the dim light from the ceiling, his hide looked milk-white and time-carved with wrinkles. His voice was sad, and I thought if I hadn't heard him talk of snakes under the big oak, it might have been even sadder. He spoke of a day of reckoning for us all and laid the truth out, mostly, which caused everyone to squirm. He spoke of worldly-ways that shocked us—well, some of us. He spoke of our greed for money. I was in that sinful bunch.

"No more!" he thundered. "No more!" He shook his feeble head. "Come Sunday, Bro. Tate will come and bring the Spirit with him!"

That allowed a week for rumors to build and build they did! Caleb said that a rumor that was sticking was that Tate was a snake-handler from the old school of Bro. Burdock and that he was probably a circuit-rider because he left ghost towns wherever he had been. He said that the "Spirit" was a rattler as long as a sawlog with buttons on his tail too many

137

to count. You wouldn't have been able to count anyway since the tail was always in a blur, and when I mentioned to Caleb that rumors like that would scare people away, he laughed. Told me that it would bring about the opposite, probably bring the church to overflow. The reason for their coming being a simple one: to see who the snake bit first! That everyone at the church would have their finger on the one they thought the snake would bite first and that they would be the only one spared. He asked to borrow fifty cents, and I loaned him a dollar, trying to get out of the sinful bunch Bro. Burdock had placed me in. Besides, it was church money, and I didn't want to leave the world without Caleb.

8

On Sunday night the congregation grew restless. Service was ready to start and Bro. Brimstone had not showed. Even Bro. Burdock seemed restless standing at the pulpit, his white hair just above the top of it. The big room was quiet as snowfall, and, I thought, the congregation a little disappointed, like they were afraid that Bro. Brimstone would not show at all. I know I was.

Looking out over the congregation from where I sat just behind the pulpit, I thought that Caleb had been right: the regulars were all there along with others who had strayed off on the mountain long ago. Cradling my guitar, I stared at people I had never seen before. All, I thought, here for the same reason—if the Spirit was a snake, to see who got bit first! I figured that my being there was a gift from here on in; no way would I be paid for my music. And yet, I wouldn't have not come for anything. I had never been more scared or excited in my life. I tried to scan the crowd and pick out who would get the snake first. But, having so many to choose from, I gave up. I tried to believe that at least two would be a sure bet to be spared: me and Bro. Burdock. Me for my music that they would need, and Bro. Burdock because he had handled snakes before. Poor Caleb would probably be first. Pitiful!

Finally, we heard the squeaking of the front door. Heads turned like a wheat field caught by a slow wind, and then Bro. Brimstone slithered through the door carrying a cage under his arm.

He was a little man, thin as a winter calf, a look of pain on his face like he had just gotten through wrestling the devil. Inside, he stopped and eyed the congregation; especially, I thought, where the boys were! And then his eyes settled on Bro. Burdock, and he nodded in recognition. He spoke; his voice started off like far-off thunder and ended up lightning: "I have come, Bro. Burdock, to gather the flock!"

Halfway up the aisle, he stopped and held the wire cage higher which gave everyone a better look at the big rattler inside, and then, swinging the cage above his head like a lantern, he thundered: "And with the help of old Penance, here they will be gathered!" He walked toward the pulpit thundering: "Penance! Penance! Penance!"

Excited, the big snake thrashed against both sides of the cage, swaying the congregation toward the wall, depending on which side of the aisle the snake was on. For me, the coming of the snake made what once seemed like a long aisle, short. Caught up in the swinging of the cage, I struck a string on my guitar by mistake and was afraid I'd have to pay for that. I felt regretful and almost sick.

Bro. Brimstone placed the cage on top of the pulpit. The snake's head was pressed against the wire, its tongue flickering like flames from a candle. And then Bro. Brimstone poked a bony finger through the wire and stroked the snake's head. That seemed to settle it considerably, which seemed to please everyone. But not for long: Brimstone stomped his foot hard on the floor and screamed: "Call me Bro. Brimstone!" And then he looked at the snake. "Penance! Penance! You are the Keys to the Kingdom! You are the Spirit! For them with faith to handle now, sinners to bide time until they're ready!"

Just when I got to thinking how nice it was for sinners to be allowed to bide time, Bro. Brimstone took the edge off of it. He thundered: "But time is short! Penance! Penance!"

Hearing its name again, the big snake thrashed the cage worse than ever, and the wire looked so thin to hold a snake that big. It hissed and hummed and fairly fought to get out of the cage. Bro. Brimstone looked down at me, and visions of my past started before my eyes again.

"Music, little sinner!" he said.

Grateful that he had picked me among the sinners, I strummed regretful and sick; miss a chord, I thought, and I could well belong to the snake. I pulled the guitar closer to my chest and tried to play soft as a feather, pretty and sad as a whippoorwill. Bro. Brimstone looked down at me with burning eyes: "Give me fire, boy, not smoke!" I strummed to nowhere and nothing. My head was full of Brimstone, my eyes full of snake! Bro. Brimstone's voice, seconded by the snake's humming rattler buttons, built the church to fever pitch. And then Bro. Brimstone opened the cage and lifted the snake out. It slid up his arm, twined around his neck, and stuck its tail about his head and sung. Bro. Brimstone stroked it and talked pretty to it. And then he stretched his arm to point over the congregation, and the rattler slid out along Brimstone's arm!

"Penance! Penance! Penance!" he thundered.

The big snake seemed on the verge of jumping off Bro. Brimstone's finger tips and biting someone in the congregation right off, thinning us the first night. The congregation swayed backwards, but then the big snake turned a loop and slithered back up Brimstone's arm. Farther away, I thought, from the congregation but closer to me! Again and again the big snake threatened to jump among the congregation, like a cat teasing mice. Bro. Brimstone's talking pretty would settle it down; a stomp on the floor would rile it up. Bro. Brimstone, using the snake's head as a pointer, shot a period on everyone among the congregation, just like the teacher at Sourwood School. The snake fought to get loose to do what it must have figured it had been brought here to do: bite everyone! Bro. Brimstone preached powerful!

To begin with, we all found out that we were worse off than even Bro. Burdock had said we were. All living on borrowed time, payment long-overdue. One moment his voice was sad and mournful, and tears ran down his lean jaws; but heat from his message built quickly, drying the tears and scorching the lot of us. He said that he hoped that he and old Penance would get to know each and every one of us, close-up, that he hoped in time to visit with us outside the church. And I was sure that there was not one among the congregation who believed he would not be bringing the snake with him. And then thinking that we'd be happy about it, he told us he hoped to be with us a long time. He might be here a long time, I thought, but for the rest of us, it depended on the snake!

At the end of his message, he lifted his arms in the air and asked for all who were prepared to handle to come forward. No one moved. And then, reminding again that there was time to bide, he asked for all sinners to come forward. The pews emptied.

"Dear Bro. Burdock," he said, "I've never seen a church so full of sin and willing to admit it. It's worse than on Blaine before I cleaned it up."

I had never been to Blaine before; I figured it was a ghost town now, and I'd never go. And then Bro. Brimstone looked down at me again. "Music, little sinner!" he said.

Appreciating what I hoped would be a nickname, I also hoped the big snake would allow for a missed chord or two.

Going back over the mountain that night was pure misery. The mountain offered so many places where a snake could hide or sneak up on you.

"Nothing to be afraid of up here," Caleb said. "Cold as it is the snake couldn't get far without hibernating."

"About how far do you think?" I asked.

"How would I know?" Caleb said. "I ain't a snake."

During the days that followed I fared no better. With my life rendered down to a snake, I thought I saw them everywhere. Caleb said I saw more snakes than Hershel. He also said the big snake would straighten Hershel out. Looking into the eyes of the snake, I had never been as scared in my life; worse yet, I was proud to be a coward and be known for it, not having to handle as long as I stayed that way.

With Mayhall gone, and no longer bound to keep the secret, I told Caleb what happened that night at the Glory Hole.

"Don't look good on Sister Elma," he said. "Most people thought she'd handle the snake right off except me. I mean, my knowing her fear of snakes from taking Hershel home. With all she's had the right to believe useless now, she'll have to handle in the end or be like the rest of us, which is gone if you don't, and gone if you do."

I even thought about giving up the church, but that meant two things: one, a certain, and the other too close to gamble on. One was that I would miss seeing who would get bit first and have a life hardly worth living, and the second was that if I was not there, Bro. Brimstone would probably come looking for me and my music. I thought of the collection plate, how full it had been. How much, I couldn't know because Bro. Brimstone was in charge of that and probably the snake guarding it.

After a few Sundays, so much money was collected that two plates were passed around. And Brimstone started a special building fund to enlarge the church which pleased Bro. Burdock greatly.

"It's turned into a sideshow," Caleb said. "Just like I said it would." So many people came now that we had to go early to find a seat or standing room. And whenever members of the congregation grumbled about it not being Christian to force people to church out of fear, Caleb said that wasn't it at all: they came the same as we did, to see who got bit first.

Bro. Burdock wallowed in it all. And why not? With Brimstone pointing out that Bro. Burdock was the way, and never being called on to handle the snake, he walked the aisle mostly now trying to coax members of the congregation to handle. The congregation dodged him like a plague, even Sister Elma. And he joined Bro. Brimstone to pass the plates along the pews, and with the big snake with them, who wouldn't give?

"Brimstone's cleaning out Sourwood Mountain," Caleb said. "Be lucky if there's a penny left when he's through. I'd like to see the size of that pot now."

Afraid that Caleb and some of the boys might try to take a look at it and I'd be too curious not to go with them, I said: "He'd have old Penance guarding it!"

"Wouldn't be worth the gamble," Caleb said.

Brimstone called for a revival, and we went every night now. And there were times when I could look at the snake, and it wouldn't sing his rattlers at me. But just when I thought it might be trying to make up, it'd try to get through the cage at me. It'd set a point on the congregation like they were a covey of quail. Everyone thought it was just a matter of time now until the first one got bit. Brimstone would turn the snake loose.

"He'll not do that," Caleb said. "He might lose it, and that snake's the mother-lode. I might catch me a snake one day and take up doing a little preaching myself."

But I knew that Caleb never would—he was as afraid of snakes as I was. My life was a shaky one, hanging by four fingers and a picking thumb! The snake was the wind in the trees and bird-shadows that fell from the sky!

To make matters worse, Bro. Brimstone said to me one night: "You ever run across a field mouse on your trapline?"

"Sometimes," I answered.

"Fetch me one," he said, "and you'll be rewarded."

Too curious not to, I asked: "That what it eats?"

Bro. Brimstone grinned, and I take oath his teeth looked shoepegged. He said: "When he ain't eating little sinners what won't bring a mouse!"

I worried myself sick. Afraid that I might not catch one, and if I did, what my reward might be! Well, I brought in the mouse; too afraid not to, too curious not to. I regretted it. The snake swallowed the poor mouse in one gulp—showing how quick a life could go!

The big rattler had made so many changes in the services, testimonies for one thing. They generally all started the same: "Lord, you know I am a sinner!"

But Brimstone and the snake brought more grumbling, too. Slaboak was now even more of a sideshow than Caleb had imagined. Outsiders who had heard about the snake handler came to see. They crowded the pews and gathered along the walls and were willing to pay for the show they saw. More collection plates were passed around. Bro. Brimstone never disappointed them. What he didn't have the snake doing wasn't worth talking about. He'd belittle us by calling members of the congregation to come handle, and when they held back, he'd threaten to sic the snake on them. He exposed our sins to the outsiders, and they laughed until they cried, but always he pointed out that Bro. Burdock was the way and that kept Burdock pacified.

On our way back over the mountain one night Caleb said: "Brimstone could be going too far. Talking about our sins and misgivings to us is one thing, telling them to outsiders is another. The congregation is grumbling bad, especially Sister Elma. He's made a fool of her, and she's got Rennie on her side."

"I'll bet Rennie ain't really afraid to handle the snake!"

143

"Rennie knows the snake would bite her quick as it would some-one else," Caleb said. "But a snake ain't got nothing to do with scrip-ture."

"Then why do they use 'em?" I asked

"There's enough people around to believe a little of everything," Caleb answered.

There were times now that even Bro. Burdock looked worried, like the church had become a spectacle that not even he could stop. Brimstone and the snake lived off in a small room tacked on the back of the church, and with a potbellied stove in the church and in his room that meant two stoves to feed day and night. That took a lot of wood; wood that was furnished from off the mountain by members of the congregation, including me and Caleb at times. He knew wood. He demanded the best: hickory, locust, oak, and beech were his favorites.

Going back over the mountain one night Caleb said: "He's gone too far! Sister Elma, Rennie, and some of the other women are plot-ting something. Brimstone is so tied up in gathering money and put-ting on a show for outsiders that he can't see it. He could be a short-timer."

"Brimstone is one thing," I said. "The snake is another!"

"Maybe so," Caleb said. "But they've formed a committee to see where the money is, and they plan to meet at Sister Elma's tomorrow night. If they can smoke him out on the money, they might have him!"

9

Caleb was right. After church service the following night, Sister Elma, Rennie, and a group of other women from the church trailed off to meet at Sister Elma's house. Caleb asked me to hang back, to stay off near the creek. He was afraid that I might get too excited and sound the alarm while he and some of the older boys sneaked close enough to her house to peep in the window and hear what was said. He got me to do that by making a promise that he would tell me what was said, and also because I wasn't sure that Bro. Brimstone hadn't found out already about the committee and might follow them with the snake. I hitched up on a high bank, hid behind some bushes, and squinted toward her house. By the light of the moon, I could see Caleb and the boys hunkered below a window. I saw Caleb raise to a half-hunker which allowed him to see in the window. With his head pressed tight against the facing, I knew that he was listening.

On our way home over the mountain that night, Caleb said that the committee had discussed how they could come up with a way for them to handle the money and leave church souls only to Bro. Brimstone. And while I could not vouch for the truth of what he told me, I was caught with a "too good not to believe and a wanting it to be so."

Knowing they would need someone to carry the message to Brimstone, they went down the list. Members of the committee were the first to be taken off. Finally, they settled on Bro. Mole Burton. On the surface, Caleb said, Bro. Mole was the right, and maybe only, choice. He thrived on attention, being inside the coal mine all day and getting so little of it. Tack some on him, and he'd generally do whatever he was asked to do. Problem with Mole was, not being able most times to remember something between the distance of two fence posts, he might forget. They knew, also, that excited, Bro. Mole always shook just this side of palsy and stuttered so badly that he was hard to understand. But he was the only one they could come up with who couldn't think fast enough to say no. To help, they figured to ask Mrs. Mole to join the committee the following night. She liked attention, too.

While I was some mad at Mole for being part of my losing my money at the pit, I felt sorry for him; I could feel sorry for anyone who might be facing old Penance. Poor Bro. Mole! Small and wiggly, he had gone to work in the belly-mines at the age of seven. Crawling inside the mine at daybreak and coming out after dark. He had spent so much of his life underground that whenever he was out in natural light he squinted and fumbled around like a mole will do. That is how he ended up with his nickname. He was married to a little woman no taller than a tomato stake, and Caleb and the other boys had named her Mrs. Mole. Maybe being around him so long, she squinted in natural light and fumbled too. Generally, you saw them together only two times a week: Saturdays and Sundays. On Saturdays they went into town to take in the picture show and buy grub to last a week, Bro.

145

Mole carrying it home in a burlap sack that he slung over his shoulder. Mrs. Mole followed behind with her head bowed like she was searching for something that had fallen out of the sack. You saw them again together on Sunday nights at church. I had heard Mom say that Bro. Mole wasn't far away from collecting his miner's pension, but if what Caleb said was true, he was closer to collecting a home where there was never any natural light—six-foot down!

The following night, I hitched up on the high bank to watch after Caleb had promised once again to tell me everything that happened. And even though Caleb never knew, I was even more willing to take the high ground. For this, I felt sure, was the night that someone was going to get bit! Caleb made sure that boys were staked out at both the house and the church. And since the beginning would be at Sister Elma's, I saw him pressed again against the window, but I could just make him out; snow clouds were stealing the light of the moon. The last I saw was the committee, with Bro. and Mrs. Mole added to it, disappear inside Sister Elma's house. All that happened from that point on I got from Caleb on our way home over the mountain.

Caleb said the way it turned out, the committee quickly voted Bro. Mole to head their committee, which pleased him just this side of palsy. He had always been used to being on the tail end of things instead of the front end.

It pleased Sister Mole, too. She twitched her nose and patted Bro. Mole on the arm. They coaxed him to approach Bro. Brimstone with the message for the committee to handle the money and leave the souls to him. Sister Elma said: "Now ain't that a nice idea, Bro. Mole!"

Heaped with praise from everyone, Bro. Mole said: "It . . . it certainly is."

Not wanting to give Bro. Mole time to think about it, they cautioned him that if Brimstone asked for names of the committee, he was to tell Brimstone that he had thought of the idea. They sent him on his way. He fumbled off toward the church where Brimstone (and the boys staked out there) would be waiting for him.

Bro. Mole wasn't gone long. He fumbled back up the path to Sister Elma's and palsied inside.

"Did you give him the message?" Sister Lottie asked.

"Lo . . . Lor . . . Lordy!" Bro. Mole stuttered.

Sister Mole patted him harder and said: "Now, now!"

Sister Elma said: "Get hold of yourself, Bro. Mole!" She squinted toward the door. "Did you give him the message?"

Bro. Mole, his head down as if he was talking to the floor, said: "I went over to the church and found Bro. Brimstone like you asked me to. I said that they's a committee what's a-wondering if it might be all right for them to handle church money and leave only the souls to you. He looks down at me with eyes lit up like carbide lights and says. . . ." He shook so badly now he had to stop.

"Now, now!" Sister Mole said, twitching her nose.

"Go on, Bro. Mole," Rennie coaxed.

Bro. Mole stuttered: "He leans down and tells me to tell the committee that he plans to take care of the money and the souls, too. 'For you see, Bro. Mole,' he says, 'I've got misgivings about anyone handling money that won't handle a snake.' Is that all, Bro. Brimstone, I asked? 'Well, no it ain't,' he says. 'For you see, Bro. Mole, I like you. I think you ought to be rewarded for bringing me word of the committee. Just close your eyes and hold out your hands. Now I know how well you can see in the dark being inside the mine all day so don't peep!' I held out my hands with my eyes shut and Lo . . . Lor . . . Lordy!"

"Now, now," Sister Mole pacified.

"Just a little farther along," Sister Elma coaxed.

Sister Mole fanned him with her bonnet.

He stuttered: "I felt something soft-like fall in my hands! 'You can look now, Bro. Mole,' he says to me, he did. And when I opened my eyes, I was looking eyeball to eyeball with old Penance! And while it twined around my arm, I saw Bro. Brimstone's teeth and wished I hadn't; they was as sharp as shoepegs! Lo . . . Lor . . . Lordy!"

"Now, now," Sister Mole said.

Sister Rennie leaned over: "The snake, Bro. Mole! The snake! Did it follow you?"

Bro. Mole lifted his hands and stared at them like he was looking to see if the snake was still there. It wasn't, but several members of the committee stood back and then circled him like Blinddog had circled Caleb's rooster, looking for particulars.

"I . . . I don't remember!" Bro. Mole answered.

"Did you give him the names of the committee?" Sister Elma said.

"I . . . I don't remember," Bro. Mole answered.

Caleb said the committee broke up without prayer!

10

But as it turned out the committee had nothing to worry about as far as Bro. Brimstone was concerned. Two days after they had met, Caleb picked off a rumor that Bro. Brimstone had left, taking the church money and Riley Sumner's wife with him, but that he had also left the snake inside the church! Church members staked the church out. When Bro. Brimstone didn't show, they set about worrying what to do with the snake still inside. He was probably among the pews by now waiting to bite someone on Sunday! Some members thought it best to wait until Saturday before looking; with no one to feed the fires, the snake ought to be hibernated from the cold by then. But, most looked off at Bro. Burdock for guidance. Ninety-seven years old and had never taken an aspirin!

When we got word that Bro. Burdock would check the church out on Saturday so that Sunday service wouldn't be missed, we all gathered there. We filled the churchyard and dotted the mountainside. Most brought something to eat and drink. Caleb said it was like a picnic!

I hunkered there with Caleb and watched Bro. Burdock crook his ninety-seven-year-old fingers around a forked stick that he had cut from the big oak and wade inside the door.

He found the snake! He also found out that it never had a tooth in its head: they had been pulled!

On Sunday, Rennie took the pulpit and told us that Bro. Burdock was down with a bad cold which gave hope to all of us! Riley Sumner testified that his wife, Effie, had left and that she had gone with Bro. Brimstone. But rumor was ahead of testimony on that! He said that his only regret was that she wouldn't have to handle the snake. Several among the congregation "Amened" that!

The next day along the mountain, I said to Caleb: "What did you think of the forked stick?"

"Didn't fool me none," he answered.

"How come?" I asked.

"I've known about a forked stick for a long time," he said. "Everyone carries one in their back pocket so they'll have two ways to go instead of one, mostly going by way of the forked stick, it being the easier of the two."

I had never thought about it that way even though I had been going that way myself—mostly.

"Caleb, you're smart!" I said.

But Caleb was squinting off toward the house now like he wanted to be sure Mom was not in sight. And then, he reached in his pocket and pulled out a plug of tobacco, knowing full well that he was going by way of the forked stick since he had swore to Mom that he didn't use tobacco at all.

"Yep," he said, "Ross Burdock made it to ninety-seven carrying one." Caleb reached the plug of tobacco toward me. "Time you learn."

Squinting to make sure Mom was out of sight and then going by way of the forked stick myself, I bit me off a chew. The Devil's cud was soft and sweet. I'd chew now and pay later.